Hello, Family Members,

Learning to read is one of the most important accomplishments of early childhood. **Hello Reader!** books are designed to help children become skilled readers who like to read. Beginning readers learn to read by remembering frequently used words like "the," "is," and "and"; by using phonics skills to decode new words; and by interpreting picture and text clues. These books provide both the stories children enjoy and the structure they need to read fluently and independently. Here are suggestions for helping your child *before*, *during*, and *after* reading:

Before

- Look at the cover and pictures and have your child predict what the story is about.
- Read the story to your child.
- Encourage your child to chime in with familiar words and phrases.
- Echo read with your child by reading a line first and having your child read it after you do.

During

- Have your child think about a word he or she does not recognize right away. Provide hints such as "Let's see if we know the sounds" and "Have we read other words like this one?"
- Encourage your child to use phonics skills to sound out new words.
- Provide the word for your child when more assistance is needed so that he or she does not struggle and the experience of reading with you is a positive one.
- Encourage your child to have fun by reading with a lot of expression ... like an actor!

After

- Have your child keep lists of interesting and favorite words.
- Encourage your child to read the books over and over again. Have him or her read to brothers, sisters, grandparents, and even teddy bears. Repeated readings develop confidence in young readers.
- Talk about the stories. Ask and answer questions. Share ideas about the funniest and most interesting characters and events in the stories.

I do hope that you and your child enjoy this book.

— Francie Alexander
Chief Education Officer,
Scholastic's Learning Ventures

For Charlotte Steiner, the original Aqua Girl!
—K.M.

To Taylor and Preston—
Thanks for the water wings.
—M.S.

ISBN 0-439-31946-3

Text copyright © 2002 by Kate McMullan.
Illustrations copyright © 2002 by Mavis Smith.
All rights reserved. Published by Scholastic Inc.
SCHOLASTIC, HELLO READER, CARTWHEEL BOOKS,
and associated logos are trademarks and/or
registered trademarks of Scholastic Inc.

Library of Congress Cataloging-in-Publication Data

McMullan, Kate.
  Fluffy learns to swim / by Kate McMullan; illustrated by Mavis Smith.
    p. cm. — (Hello reader! Level 3)
  Summary: At the beach with Wade's family, Fluffy the guinea pig can't seem to convince anyone that pigs don't swim, and he even has doubts himself after dreaming that he is Aqua Pig.
  ISBN 0-439-31946-3
      [1. Guinea pigs—Fiction. 2. swimming—Fiction.] I. Smith, Mavis, ill. II. Title. III. Series.
PZ7.M2295 Fe 2002   2001049413
[E]—dc21
10 9 8 7 6 5 4   04 05 06

Printed in the U.S.A.   23
First printing, May 2002

About the Author

Jo Kinnard lives with her husband, Mike, and their two dogs in Antioch, Illinois. She has been a K–12 teacher as well as a college professor. She was deeply involved with implementing the electronic portfolio program at Clayton College and State University, Georgia, and has been working with cutting-edge educational technologies since 1989.

Preface

This book is for anyone who wants to discover the teacher within oneself through the creation of a teacher portfolio. If you are a student in a teacher education program, or an in-service teaching professional building a teacher portfolio for the first time, this book is especially for you. As the title indicates, you will gain an in-depth understanding of the teacher portfolio process and be able to build your first teacher portfolio—traditional or electronic—using the guidelines and examples provided.

The value of building a teacher portfolio is now well recognized. Several books have been written on this topic, and some offer suggestions on how to go about building a portfolio. While the material in these books is valuable, there continues to be a gray area containing questions that have not been fully addressed, making it difficult for the first-time portfolio builder to get past the initial hurdles: Is my portfolio a detailed CV? What must a reflection contain? Is this item good enough for a portfolio artifact? How can I make my portfolio look convincing as evidence of my skills? This book is an attempt to clear the mist and answer such questions.

The highly reflective and participative activity of building a teacher portfolio requires an immersion and commitment to the process on the part of both portfolio owners and reviewers, along with opportunities for both sides to share helpful pointers and examples along the way. The fact that technology is a given in today's world sometimes makes it hard to remember that digital tools and software are not an end but a means to learning. In this book I want to show how you can build a teacher portfolio and grow as a teacher, effectively utilizing the opportunities provided by technology. I also want to help you see that the unavoidably digital nature of our world today can be turned to our advantage. If this book has accomplished its purpose, you will see your teacher portfolio as a living and breathing entity, one that grows you and grows with you.

MY JOURNEY

Writing this book expresses my own journey as a teacher—from my first jobs (drama teacher for grades 2 through 8 and French teacher for grades 8 through

12) where I taught without using technology, to my active involvement with teaching technologies within and outside of my classroom.

My explorations with the uses of digital technology in education began in the late eighties when I became involved in an exciting project to bring Logo and other software languages to the K–12 classroom. Inspired by Papert's book *Mindstorms* (Seymour Papert, *Mindstorms: Children, Computers and Powerful Ideas*. New York: Basic Books, 1980), I joined the ranks of educators all over the globe seeking ways to use technology to spark learning "discoveries" in K–12 children. A few years earlier I had learned several programming languages, and as I got swept into the movement for technology in education, the philosopher in me began to see the awesome conceptual connections made possible by using the right tools. In the years that followed, I watched from the perspective of student, teacher, and parent as the world became increasingly networked and digitized.

Armed with a Ph.D. in Philosophy and a teaching background, I found myself at Temple University, Pennsylvania, in the mid-nineties pursuing an M.S. in Computer Science, and teaching writing, critical reading, logic, and philosophy part-time. When Temple started its Teaching, Learning, and Technology Committee, I was fortunate to be a part of it. I was offered the opportunity to conduct a university-wide survey—sponsored by this committee and the Office of the Provost—on how professors in different disciplines were teaching with technology. I met with, interviewed, and observed professors considered to be "early adopters" of teaching technologies. Some taught online courses as "virtual professors" while others used bulletin boards, listservs, and chat programs that encouraged students in a particular course to continue their dialogues outside the classroom. This research gave me an up-close and personal view of the digital revolution from a teaching and learning perspective. It was an inspiring and exciting time in my life. I also got to try some of these tools in my own teaching to experience them firsthand. It was clear that digital technology had the potential for deepening our teaching and learning experiences in a multitude of ways. I continued my work in this direction when I served as a faculty member with the Teaching, Learning, and Technology Committee at Rowan College of New Jersey (now Rowan University). I did not know it then, but the electronic portfolio revolution was waiting around the corner.

In 2002, as a professor at Clayton College and State University, Georgia, I got involved with designing the electronic portfolio program for graduating seniors in the Bachelor of Information Technology program. Serving on the school's electronic portfolio implementation committee, I worked closely with the teaching improvement center and the Teacher Education and Business schools in defining the value of the portfolio for aspiring teachers and other professionals. I became an active spokesperson for the use of electronic portfolios, welcoming opportunities to talk to students and fellow professors about the portfolio process in classes, workshops, and more formal settings. It was exciting to help others see electronic portfolio software as a versatile tool to carry forward the core values of the portfolio process to new levels of understanding about teaching, in a networked world. Shortly thereafter, I started work on this book.

FEATURES OF THIS BOOK

In a nutshell, the book offers the following features:

- A straightforward explanation of the portfolio process in teacher education
- A practical approach to building a teacher portfolio
- Answers to questions about building a teacher portfolio
- Samples of portfolio artifacts
- A self-inquiry process for the portfolio owner to refine his or her reflection skills
- Suggestions for making the teacher portfolio a unique and living document
- A guided tour of electronic portfolio software and its applications
- Examples from student and in-service portfolios

YOUR JOURNEY

From the perspective of chapter content, the book is laid out as follows:

- Chapter 1 starts by setting out assumptions and defining this book's audience.
- Chapter 2 provides an optional historical background of the development and use of portfolios in teaching.
- Chapter 3 conducts an in-depth examination of what constitutes a portfolio artifact, and offers the reader a self-inquiry process to use in gathering and refining artifacts. It also looks at some universally accepted standards for artifacts, and answers questions that the portfolio owner may have about the process.
- Chapter 4 steps back and takes a bird's eye view of the portfolio as a whole, addressing different sections of the portfolio.
- Chapter 5 zooms back in and examines the reflective nature of the portfolio process. It also puts the portfolio owner in the shoes of a portfolio reviewer.
- Chapter 6 introduces the reader to electronic portfolio software, and provides a tour of its features and possibilities.
- Chapter 7 shares samples from the portfolios of a student teacher and an in-service teacher.

I hope these pages express my passion and love for teaching, and my personal quest as a lifelong learner. I also hope the book inspires you to find the many dimensions of your own inner teacher.

ACKNOWLEDGMENTS

I want to thank the following individuals and outstanding teachers, all of whom contributed freely of their time and energy—some in reviewing the manuscript and giving me vital suggestions for making this an effective book, and others in sharing their teaching experiences with me: Royce Robertson, Plymouth State University; Katharine Cummings, Western Michigan University; G. Nathan Carnes, University of South Carolina; Richard Carriveau, Black Hills State University; Kelly M. Costner, Wingate University; Lynne Ensworth, University of Northern Iowa; Debra Adrian Heiss, Cardinal Stritch University; James Hewitt, Saginaw Valley State University; Joy Hines, Southeastern Louisiana University; Dennis Holt, University of North Florida; David Keiser, Montclair State University; Barbara J. Moore, Mississippi University of Women; Ronghua Ouyang, Kennesaw State University; Anne Marie Tryjankowski, Saint Bonaventure University; and Jeanne Tunks, University of North Texas.

Last but not least, I want to acknowledge my gratitude to my husband, Mike, for his support, encouragement, and constructive feedback.

TO THE INSTRUCTOR

The software license included with this book is limited to the "OWNER" role of iWebfolio and is intended to enable individuals to create their own portfolios. There are several references to the "REVIEWER" role of iWebfolio throughout this text, which is not included in this software license.

The REVIEWER role of iWebfolio enables faculty to create templates and measures that can be shared with their students, and supports better organization of the process of review and feedback provided to each individual. In addition, the REVIEWER role enables measurement and feedback data to be extracted from a collection of portfolios for program level-assessment.

For more information or to acquire a software license for the REVIEWER role, please contact:

sales@nuventive.com
(877) 366-8700

Teacher Portfolios—the Journey Begins

AUDIENCE AND ASSUMPTIONS

If you are a student in a teacher education program, you are aware that the teacher portfolio (or teaching portfolio as it is sometimes called) is an important part of the assessment of your progress in the program. If you are a teaching professional starting your first portfolio, you may be working to fulfill a new promotion or tenure requirement. You may have many questions about the portfolio process. You may have seen the teacher portfolios of other novice teachers further along in the program or read the institutional guidelines for teacher portfolios in your program. This book will provide you with the answers and guidelines you need to turn your teacher portfolio from a concept into a reality, and get you moving on your professional journey.

Indeed, the construction of a teacher portfolio by the student in a teacher education program is now universally regarded as an essential step in the process of teacher certification. With the teacher portfolio being regarded as a tool of immense value for professional development, more and more in-service teachers and professors in teacher education programs are engaged in their own career-long portfolio-building. At many universities, the teacher portfolio is now a tool used for promotion and tenure across all disciplines.

Portfolios are used in several academic and nonacademic fields today, including art, business, IT, health, and architecture. They serve many purposes, such as the showcasing of professional accomplishments, individual assessment, and institutional assessment. In teacher education, portfolios represent a rich and interactive process that combines the uses mentioned above and often transcends them.

The idea of building a teacher portfolio came from Lee Shulman, who was a professor at Michigan State University in the 1970s and deeply involved in research on teaching. Shulman and his colleagues argued against the prevailing theory that teaching was a kind of skilled behavior or procedure that could be followed to get predictable results. To Shulman, teaching was the free and creative exercise of deciding how best to present a topic given the students' level of preparation, materials available, and any other immediate conditions within which learning needed to happen. Shulman helped form the Teacher Improvement Project (TAP) at Stanford in 1985, and the teacher portfolio evolved directly out of that work. Shulman viewed the teacher portfolio as a "broad metaphor that comes alive as you begin to formulate the theoretical orientation to teaching that is most valuable to you."[1] By the time you have built your teacher portfolio, you will have gathered a good deal of appreciation for Shulman's words.

If you are as passionate about teaching as I am, you can probably remember some awesome teachers who inspired you and piqued your desire to learn. Still, it's not easy to say exactly what made their teaching so effective. You may also remember a few teachers whose techniques were a reminder of what *not* to do as a teacher. One of the most effective teachers I recall from my days as a student taught a Symbolic Logic course that was a program requirement. Teaching a subject such as Logic is not a cakewalk, but Professor Bill Wisdom made it look easy. Bill seemed to have an arsenal of creative strategies for conveying the most abstract of concepts. Intertwined among the proofs that Bill's students had to write were magical moments with the Wizard of Oz, Alice in Wonderland, and even a banjo tune or two. Professor Wisdom would encourage the class to ask questions, and then offer suggestions that would somehow lead the students to find the solution. His explanations were couched in the most down-to-earth examples. His quizzes were set up to let you learn and have fun while you were about it. Bill had the rare ability to tune in to the students' level of understanding. In addition, Bill's course content was planned so well that all of the required material in the syllabus was covered in depth and on schedule. From watching his interactions with the children of students who sometimes accompanied their parents to class, it was obvious that Bill was equally effective with a six-year-old as with teenagers and adults.

As you gear up for a teaching career, you may have flashbacks of your K–12 schooling and remember the inspiring words and actions of a teacher who was a mentor to you. We know that great teachers possess an intangible quality—a mixture of qualities such as knowledge, commitment, caring, and sensitivity—that makes them effective in the communication of ideas. Take a moment to ponder the characteristics of your favorite teacher. Was it the way the teacher commanded attention? Was it the teacher's style of classroom management? Was it the way the teacher led from one idea into the next? Was it his or her ability to combine current examples and humor to serve up appealing contextual explanations? The sci-fi term "teacherbot" describes "a robot or expert system that teaches humans or other sapiens by adapting to their intelligence levels, interests, and motivations."[2] Picture the most sophisticated teacherbot imaginable— one that could mimic your mentor's every teaching move. You know somehow that it would fall short of your expectations.

The bottom line is that we may be able to state in broad terms the qualities and characteristics that separate great teachers from mediocre ones, but the complex nature of the teaching experience cannot be reduced to a set of fail-safe instructions that work for everyone in all teaching situations. Thus assessing the novice teacher's professional readiness presents quite a challenge. It involves much more than tests gauging subject knowledge or an understanding of developmental psychology, although these two areas would be a good place to start. When you talk to an experienced teacher about their first taste of teaching, you may be surprised when they tell you that the real world was not quite how they had expected it to be; that they had almost thrown in the towel in their first year; that their student teaching had not prepared them sufficiently for what lay ahead. Educators have been grappling for decades with the problem of finding reliable methods for new teacher assessment—methods that would narrow the gap between expectations and reality when the novice teacher stepped into his or her first real classroom. The possibilities opened up by the use of teacher portfolios have made them an increasingly popular teacher assessment tool. The novice may start out with the idea that his or her teacher portfolio is little more than a rite of passage to graduation from the teacher-certification program. It is not until one starts building a teacher portfolio that one realizes that there are many dimensions to the portfolio process. What exactly is a teacher portfolio and how hard is it to build one?

We live in a "plug and play" world, but despite the emergence of nifty electronic portfolio software, building a portfolio is not a plug and play process. At first glance, a teacher portfolio appears to be nothing more than a compilation of "artifacts" or required items that will provide evidence of your competencies. These items could come from a wide variety of sources and media. This book will help you see your teacher portfolio as a tool that lets you capture the essence of successful teaching, the intangible quality referred to earlier, in your own unique way. It will grow with you as you grow into a teacher, and will become a creative pursuit that ranges over a significant part of your life. As a conscious, reflective activity, it will engage you, your mentors, your students, and everyone who may be involved in your professional growth. Excited? Let's start with a brief roadmap of the next hundred or so pages.

ROADMAP OF THE BOOK

The chapter following this introduction, Chapter 2, gives a short background account of the history of teacher portfolios as an assessment tool in teacher education. You will see why portfolio building makes such a huge difference in the quality of the teaching experience. You will learn about the movement from "teacher-centered" to "student-centered" instruction, and its implications for education in the world in which we live today. If you feel you already have a deep understanding of the need for teacher portfolios and are anxious to get started on your portfolio, you may choose to start directly with Chapter 3. On the other hand, if you are still unsure about the value of teacher portfolios, Chapter 2 will explain the rationale behind the whole portfolio process. Understanding and internalizing this rationale will be critical to the quality of your portfolio, and is important as a prerequisite to starting on your portfolio. Teaching is not formulaic, and neither is building a portfolio. If nothing else, Chapter 2 will help you distinguish between a true teacher portfolio and a teacher scrapbook, and help steer your portfolio away from becoming the latter.

In Chapter 3, we drill down to the core of your teacher portfolio and discuss the concept of the portfolio artifact. The Information Age and the Internet have altered the teaching experience and placed new demands on students and teachers. Your teacher portfolio must reflect your ability to meet these demands through carefully selected artifacts. In this chapter, you will begin to ask the questions that will help you select your artifacts. We use broadly accepted standards for teacher certification to provide a background for this exploration.

Chapter 4 examines different categories of portfolio content, and explains how there are three phases in the building of a teacher portfolio. At this stage, you start to lay out the design for your teacher portfolio and a reasonable plan for its completion. This chapter includes a look at such content as personal data, the statement of your teaching philosophy, and your mission statement.

Chapter 5 switches gears and examines the portfolio from a deeper, more reflective perspective. You move past the artifact selection process to the key role of the artifact in honing your teaching skills. Chapter 5 also talks about reviewer feedback, and gives you a better understanding of the mentor role so that you and your mentor can fully benefit from the portfolio process through meaningful critique and feedback. You also learn how to recognize and understand your school's particular portfolio emphasis and use that knowledge to build a portfolio that meets your program's goals.

Chapter 6 introduces you to electronic portfolios and handy electronic portfolio software that can greatly simplify the logistical elements of building a portfolio. It also addresses some unique benefits of using electronic portfolio software, and enables you to fully utilize the features available.

Chapter 7 looks at samples of portfolio artifacts that might belong in a pre-service teacher portfolio and those that might belong in an in-service teacher portfolio. It also addresses the cultural changes wrought by our understanding of the universal value of building a portfolio. It provides a reflective look back on what you have accomplished and offers a sneak peak at what may lie ahead on your continuing professional journey.

The use of the teacher portfolio as an assessment tool for teacher education implies the acceptance of certain assumptions. Let's examine these assumptions.

ASSUMPTIONS ABOUT USING PORTFOLIOS

We make the following assumptions about the portfolio process:

- The portfolio will be developed over the course of the program and will be an expression of sustained work by the novice teacher toward meeting program and personal teaching goals.

- The portfolio will exemplify collaboration and interactive exchanges in different teaching scenarios.

- The portfolio is a setting for the novice teacher to find his or her teaching philosophy through his or her everyday practice.

- The portfolio is an opportunity for the novice teacher to benefit from a coaching and mentoring process through the feedback and discussions generated by artifacts and their accompanying reflections.

- The portfolio is an avenue for teacher identity development and represents not one singular thought process but the evolution of his or her teaching philosophy and practice as it develops from classroom practice.

- The portfolio includes the novice teacher's documented experiences along with his or her reflections on them, his or her conversations with peers and mentors, and subsequent cogitations in his or her professional growth.

- The portfolio, in essence, represents the teacher in his or her development as a lifelong learner.

It is important for us to keep in mind that despite sharing several of the assumptions listed above, each institution brings its own unique history and culture to bear upon its teacher portfolio program. While two institutions may agree on the immense value of the portfolio process, they may differ on several issues. Consider the following questions, and where necessary, bring them up with your supervisors or program administrators to get the clarification you need from the unique perspective of your teacher education program.

- **On artifacts:** Where do portfolio artifacts come from? What constitutes an artifact? Are portfolio artifacts drawn from work previously completed by the candidate, or are they deliverables expressly created for inclusion in the portfolio, or a mixture of both? Will some artifacts be required by the program and other optional artifacts be selected for inclusion by the candidate? Or will the institution require categories but allow the candidate to select the artifact or artifacts for each category? Will one or more teacher education program courses be tied to portfolio artifacts, such as research papers or studies?

- **On templates:** Is the candidate required to use an institutional template? Will this template be a loose guideline allowing for creative interpretation, a detailed and precise set of instructions that will provide uniformity in candidate templates, or some happy blend of the two?

As the appeal for portfolio-based assessment gathers momentum in teacher education as well as in other disciplines, more questions present themselves for consideration: Is a portfolio ever "complete"? Is the teacher portfolio a process, a product, or both? If the emphasis is on process, the portfolio could contain multiple versions of the same artifact, such as a lesson plan illustrating the candidate's progress and development over a period of time. However, this is not a requirement for a process-oriented portfolio. Even though a school may view their portfolio program as process-oriented, it may not always be possible, for logistical reasons, to include examples of the same artifact showing development over time. If the portfolio is to be an assessment of the candidate or teacher at a given point in his or her professional history, with artifacts showcasing skills gathered at that point, the portfolio could be viewed as having a "product" emphasis. A hybrid of the process and product approaches takes the best features of both in the assessment of the teacher or candidate's proficiencies. Here, the portfolio would include artifacts that show accomplishment in some areas and ongoing development in other areas. Music education professionals Campbell and Brummett offer a good discussion of this topic.[3] The orientation of this book is toward the latter approach. The value of the teacher portfolio process forms the primary rationale for this book, while the value of the portfolio as a reliable way to showcase a teacher's strengths is an added benefit.

SUMMARY

This introductory chapter has tried to clarify the nature of this book, the audience for whom it is intended, and the assumptions it makes about the teacher portfolio. Here are a few more points to ponder as you get ready for your own portfolio explorations.

> How do you feel about your own quest for teacher certification? How would you know (or how did you know) you were ready to be a teaching professional?

> Why is it so important for you to have an active role in your own teacher-certification process?

> Should teacher candidates be allowed to participate in the teacher-certification process of their fellow candidates?

> What is your school's primary rationale for using portfolios as a teacher-assessment tool?

ENDNOTES

1. Shulman, L. (1998). "Teacher Portfolios: A Theoretical Activity." In N. Lyons (Ed.), *With Portfolio in Hand: Validating the New Teacher Professionalism* (p. 25). New York, NY: Teachers College Press.

2. Retrieved August 2, 2005, from: http://www.orionsarm.com/glossary.html#t.

3. Campbell, M. R., and Brummett, V. M. (2002, November). *Music Educators Journal.* Retrieved December 29, 2005, from http://infotrac.thomsonlearning.com.

2

Teacher Portfolios—
a Background
Account

INTRODUCTION

This chapter provides a historical background and reinforces the reasons for using teacher portfolios as a key assessment methodology. If you are new to portfolio building in general, or are interested in knowing more about the evolution of interest in portfolio-based assessment of teachers, this chapter will provide you with valuable information. Understanding the need for teacher portfolios is closely tied to understanding the nature of the teaching process. Teaching is a complex activity that is highly dependent on context. This makes it difficult to quantify or calibrate the teacher candidate's preparedness for his or her new professional life. A teaching strategy that is very effective with one group of students could be a miserable flop with another. So in helping prepare you for your teaching career, your supervisors will ply you not just with knowledge but also with innumerable opportunities to practice your new skills—through discussions, scenarios, and actual classroom experiences. The activity of building a teacher portfolio not only lets you participate in your assessment, but is itself a learning opportunity. It allows you to revisit and share the ideas, discussions, classroom activities, and lessons you experience in the course of your program or career. The main focus of this chapter is to illustrate the intricate, fluid nature of teaching, and the way portfolios let you maximize learning (how to teach) from each teaching situation in which you are involved. Once you see this, you will find it easier to select artifacts for your teacher portfolio that capture the hard-to-measure but core aspects of your teaching.

THE ESSENCE OF TEACHING

A Scenario

If you wanted to teach middle-school children about immigration in the 1900s, how would you go about it? Read the relevant chapter aloud to the class? Take the children on a field trip to the Statue of Liberty National Monument (if you live in the area)? Hand out sheets with facts and figures? Ask students to share their family history? Hand out a research assignment on these words from the Emma Lazarus poem *The New Colossus*?

> "Give me your tired, your poor, Your huddled masses yearning to breathe free"[1]

Thanks to the Internet, these days there are many resources for ideas on teaching any given topic, such as the National Endowment for the Humanities (NEH) Web site,[2] where you can find lesson plans for language arts, culture, and history. While there is no single "correct" way to cover a chapter or topic, you may choose not to use one of the ways mentioned above, or use a combination of them depending on the ethnic composition of your class, the resources at your disposal, the content of the preceding lessons, or the skill level of the participants, to state a few of the factors you will use in preparing your lesson plan. For instance, if you were able to take the students on a field trip to the monument, you might start by inviting your students to talk about what they observed on their field trip. Put yourself in this scenario.

At first your students are shy and unwilling to talk. Slowly, you get the children engaged in an animated discussion about the plaque at the Statue of Liberty National Monument bearing the Lazarus quote, and then about life in America during the times the poem was written. Your interest and caring for the students' opinions engenders a secure learning environment in which even the shy ones can speak without fearing ridicule. Your guidance keeps the discussion from losing its thread, and the class ends on a high note. As you listen, amazed at the children's perspectives and insights, you also get a better understanding of each student's strengths and needs. You feel energized by what has been a fun class activity. You and your students have learned a lot and moved outside the facts or figures on immigration to a better understanding of cultural diversity and what each student brings to the class. You have also been the vehicle of a transformation in a child's search for identity— in the realization that there are many ways to think about something, each valid and worth being heard. You were in the teacher role, but were a learner too, in this process. Each student participated in this discovery, some more than others. In the days that follow, you help your students write and revise their research papers. You also provide verbal feedback in one-on-one dialogues where needed, until eventually the activity concludes and you move on to the next segment. Later in the year, the students' essays along with the notes you have kept will serve as examples of an activity in your teacher practice that worked well.

William Butler Yeats once said, "Education is not the filling of a pail but the lighting of a fire."[3] If your fire has been lit, you want to do the same for your students. The imaginary scenario we just discussed shows how good teachers are anything but formulaic in applying the general principles of education. But how have our general assumptions and beliefs about teaching (and consequently our methods of teacher assessment) evolved over the past fifty years?

THE TEACHING EVOLUTION

Every generation of American educators has contained thought leaders who have shaped the evolution of teaching practice, but the predominant paradigm in use in classrooms from the early 1900s through the 1980s was "teacher-centered" instruction.[4] Larry Cuban, Shulman's colleague at Stanford and a scholar in the field of teaching research in his own right, lists the following as observable measures of this model of teaching: teacher talk exceeding student talk, minimal small-group interaction, restricted movement in the classroom, and instructor-determined use of class time. Today an alternative approach described as "student-centered" is much more common. Measures of student-centered instruction are: as much or more student talk than teacher talk, a lot more small-group activity, activities of different kinds, student involvement in deciding what will be covered and for how long, students having a say in what constitutes acceptable classroom behavior, and a lot more movement within the classroom. So applying this distinction to our imaginary scenario, if you had handled the class as described, you would be leaning toward a student-centered methodology. If you were more inclined to give a lecture on immigration or have students read aloud sections from a book, you would be following a teacher-centered model of instruction. Keep in mind that even if the student-centered model seems appealing in this scenario, there may be times when the teacher-centered approach is more effective.

There were a number of reasons why teacher-centered teaching models may have endured despite alternative approaches proposed by school reform movements. Teacher-centered instruction was convenient and easier to plug into a statistics-based standard of teacher evaluation. For instance, one might evaluate a teacher's performance by the percentage of his or her students making a score of 90 percentile or above on a standardized test. It also fit in with the view (which Shulman criticized) that teaching can be analyzed into a set of discrete acts or behaviors. So in theory, if you followed the "good teaching behaviors," you could become a good teacher. The young science of educational psychology at the time emphasized such practices as rote memorization and repetition. A shortage of teachers may have forced a poor teacher-student ratio, resulting in forced economies of scale and the adoption of certain uniform teaching methods. There may also have been a widespread reluctance to adopt less-structured teaching models because it was harder to validate their effectiveness using standardized testing methodologies. To some thinkers, schools were primarily a means for social control and a way to instill desired social behaviors in a competitive society. In a teacher-centered classroom the natural leaders would supposedly "bubble" to the top.

Student-centered instruction, inspired by the ideas of thinkers such as Dewey, was based on providing equal learning opportunities in less restrictive learning conditions. It appears to have existed in pockets from the early 1900s, but mostly in small private schools. By the 1940s, student-centered classrooms were much more common in public schools, but had not yet challenged the predominant model. Some high schools were closely tied to vocational schools. Here the emphasis was on producing manpower to assume roles in the many needed hands-on professions. Others were college-prep institutions. As there exists today, even back then there was a dichotomy between classical education and vocational training. In either case, a high school classroom was more likely to be teacher-centered than student-centered. Elementary schools, on the other hand, could accommodate less-structured approaches to teaching, being some-what more removed from the responsibilities of impending adulthood. Student-centered approaches were more common in elementary schools. However, by the eighties, changes were definitely in the air. Much more credence was about to be given to student-centered instruction.

The ethnic composition of the American classroom had changed to include white, black, Hispanic, and other cultural backgrounds. The "open classroom" movement of the 1970s was more widely accepted, fostering such educational thought constructs as active, student-initiated, self-directed learning.[5] Assumptions about learning were changing, and the public at large was about to demand more from schools than they had hitherto been able to provide.

THE DEMAND FOR SCHOOL REFORM

The late 1970s and early 1980s marked a period characterized by strident demands for school reform and an increasing impatience on the part of the public with what they saw as a failing educational system. In 1981, Secretary of Education T. H. Bell responded by creating the National Commission on Excellence in Education (NCEE) to look into the widespread public discontent with American education. Members of the NCEE were prominent educators drawn from schools and universities across the country. In April 1983, the NCEE completed its charge by submitting a report entitled *A Nation at Risk*.[6] The paper's findings came from a broad base of information gathered from polls, papers by experts on educational programs, and testimony from parents, teachers, students, business leaders, public groups, and scholars at public hearings, panel discussions, and symposia.

The paper outlined the serious decline in America's status as the unchallenged world leader in commerce, industry, science, and technology. American students' achievements in tests compared poorly with the achievements of students from other industrialized nations. Functional illiteracy ran high in both adults and youth. SAT scores had continued to decline. Forty percent of 17-year-olds were lacking in higher order thinking skills. Companies found that they needed to spend a lot of money on remedial education for their workers, who failed to meet even the most basic standards. These statistics painted a very gloomy picture for the future of American world leadership, particularly when the use of technology in all fields was booming. So even though the average citizen was better educated in 1983 than his or her counterpart from a generation earlier, there had been a decline in standards compared to three decades ago. The root cause of this decline, the paper alleged, was the mediocre state of the educational system, no longer adequate to fend off international competition in any field. It went on to stress that unless a high-quality education was made freely available to every American, the country would lose its superiority in the Information Age. It is interesting to note that some of these concerns are still valid today.

The paper demanded school reform that would enable each individual to learn more and do better in school, and become a lifelong learner. This emphasis on the individual would then contribute to the development of a "learning society" once more able to lead the world. The paper revealed that the public placed education above healthcare, welfare, and military defense as critical to the strength and security of the nation.

The need for urgent school reform led to the recognition that producing better teachers by raising standards for teacher certification (not merely expecting better student performance) was the real starting point for improving the educational system. The emphasis shifted from a preoccupation with test scores to finding better ways of assessing student teacher progress and thereby ushering in an era of professional respectability for teachers. To produce good teachers, there needed to be a tool that would better serve the intricate, interactive, and creative act of teaching, and this tool would have to be situational and contextualized rather than purely statistical. This new tool would be the teacher portfolio.[7] The work of pioneers such as Shulman and newly created organizations such as the National Board for Professional Teaching Standards (NBPTS) and the Interstate New Teacher Assessment and Support Consortium (INTASC) in examining new and improved criteria for teacher certification led to the adoption of the teacher portfolio as a viable teacher assessment methodology. It was by this time becoming increasingly clear that relying heavily on tests as a method of assessment would not work for teacher certification programs. While those tests might work well for assessing an individual's subject knowledge, they lacked features crucial to a profession entrusted with the care of future generations.

The use of teacher portfolios started with the belief that prevailing teacher assessment methods were insufficient to ensure professionalism in teaching. Under the teacher-centered model of instruction, the teacher's compliance with the "teacher rulebook" could easily be evaluated.[8] However, if teachers were expected to be active creators of constructive learning environments, rather than merely performing a set of prescribed behaviors, their performance could no longer be tracked on a checklist. There needed to be some way to capture the teacher's ability to build contexts that would foster learning. The teacher would have to demonstrate her deep understanding of the subject as well as show that her understanding went beyond mere subject knowledge. She would need to show that she could alter her handling of a subject based on the learner's inhibitions, fears, and prior learning. She would need to be able to explain concepts in a number of ways and be able to address individual learning needs. The teacher portfolio provided a convenient platform upon which these abilities could be assessed. In it the teacher could a) document his teaching methods in a student-centered classroom, b) share his teaching philosophy with examples, c) provide samples of student work resulting from such teaching, d) engage in case studies of particular students or the application of particular teaching methods, e) write down reflections on one's experiences, and f) record interactions with mentors and peers—to name a few of the myriad uses of the portfolio. The question foremost on many educators' minds was: would the portfolio deliver on its promise or would it be little more than a glorified scrapbook?

PORTFOLIOS, NOT SCRAPBOOKS

As mentioned earlier, portfolios are used in programs other than teacher education. For example, an information technology major may be required to submit a senior portfolio that includes samples of work completed in different courses taken during the course of her progress through the degree program. Even in its most simple implementation, this type of portfolio can be valuable in several ways. First, the fresh graduate can showcase her skills to potential employers. The portfolio offers concrete evidence of skills acquired and training completed in core areas. Second, a feedback section on each assignment in the portfolio can be required by the school. This feedback section can be used to share peer and mentor comments on different aspects of the assignment. To take the process even further, adding a reflection section would allow valuable insights to be captured pertaining to content, project management, and group dynamics. From a school perspective, valuable feedback about the success of the program in meeting its goals could be gathered from the portfolio reviews of the students in the program, and this process could be formalized to the degree desired. The portfolio becomes a vehicle for fostering lifelong learners, who will then take this quality into the workplace, engendering the creation of a learning society. Using portfolios in a teacher education program further multiplies these advantages because of the inherently communicative and reflective nature of teaching and learning. So the answer to the question of whether portfolios are little more than glorified scrapbooks becomes a categorical "No!"

To illustrate this, let's "fast forward" for a bit to a snapshot further on in your teacher education program. You are working on building your teacher portfolio. The portfolio will contain many different artifacts. At the moment, you are looking for samples of student work from completed assignments that you considered especially insightful and productive in the context of your development as a teacher. You rediscover the essay assignment on the Statue of Liberty Monument field trip, and decide that it must be included in your portfolio.

Over the course of your program, and later on when you rebuild your teacher portfolio as a certified professional, you find that this artifact (and every other well-chosen portfolio artifact) is a "gift that keeps on giving." Each time you review your notes from the class discussions and the dialogues with individual students, you see in them new opportunities for learning. As you revisit the essays, your mind starts to make fresh connections and you see the assignment in a new light. You capture ideas for future assignments. Reading Bobby's essay reminds you of his quiet, thoughtful approach to the essay and the revisions that had been made before the final submission. Jordan's essay is strikingly different and handles the same subject in a more exuberant fashion. You remember her excitement on the field trip and in the class discussion and how little it took to get her to talk about anything. Each student sample reminds you about the child's unique way of learning.

You begin to see how the same essay topic can be used as a launching pad for a study of pie charts: of all the people who immigrated to the United States in the year 1920, what percentage were from Italy? What percentage of new immigrants were farmers? Each time you teach the same segment, you are able to add a new richness to your presentation, drawing from your reflections on the times before. The artifacts in your portfolio give you insights about your own teaching philosophy, and you use this self-assessment to forge your professional identity. So in a nutshell, your well-constructed teacher portfolio is far more than a scrapbook. It becomes the venue where you will capture and showcase your past and future potential as a teacher. Instead of merely relying on your students' performance in a multiple-choice test as an indicator of your teaching skills, the educators in your teacher-education program can use concrete situational examples of your skills as manifested in your portfolio artifacts.

Coming Full Circle

Working on your portfolio can make you a better teacher and at the same time offer you a way to showcase your skills for certification, promotion, and tenure. Teaching, in Shulman's words, "is thought and action with regard to children, purposes, and content in particular contexts."[9] Teacher assessment has to take that context into consideration in order to be meaningful. The "one size fits all" approach to teacher assessment simply does not make sense. Payne's words (in his book on applied educational assessment) express the fundamental argument for the use of portfolios as an assessment mechanism (whether it is for school children or teacher candidates): " . . . the major advantage in using portfolios as performance assessments is in the involvement and investment of the student in a process that directly relates to instruction."[10] The teacher portfolio works because it lets the candidate assume an integral role in the assessment mechanism. However, we have to guard against a dilution of the portfolio process. It is easy to turn a portfolio into a scrapbook if all it contains are discrete examples of teaching without a connecting strand or thread running through them. The portfolio can also become a scrapbook if it is no more than a "Me, Myself, and I" account. To realize their potential, portfolios need to be a truthful representation of the teacher's development over a period of time with emphasis on learning. This would mean including examples of the teacher candidate's successful and not-so-successful classroom experiences.

Selecting artifacts for your portfolio is an involved process, but one that is made vastly easier when you comprehend the process and are invested in it. Now, let's get to it and start building!

SUMMARY

In this first chapter, we explored the nature of the teaching process and examined the origin of the use of teacher portfolios as an assessment tool. We listed assumptions about the teacher portfolio, and explained why it holds so much promise. Finally, we set the stage for providing situational examples relating to teaching and the process of building a teacher portfolio.

Here are some points to ponder. Perhaps they will provide a starting point for your own portfolio explorations.

Examining teacher certification standards today, do you feel we have gotten closer to the idea of a learning society?

Why were the early adopters of portfolio assessment of teacher candidates so dissatisfied with other more prevalent teacher-assessment methods?

ENDNOTES

1. Academy of American Poets. (n.d.). Retrieved July 31, 2005, from http://www.poets.org/viewmedia.php/prmMID/16111.

2. The following National Endowment for the Humanities (NEH) site gives detailed suggestions for such an activity and other related activities. Retrieved July 31, 2005, from http://edsitement.neh.gov/view_lesson_plan.asp?id=351.

3. Retrieved October 9, 2005, from http://www.brainyquote.com/quotes/quotes/w/williambut101244.html.

4. Cuban, L. (2004). *How Teachers Taught: Constancy and Change in American Classrooms 1890–1980*. New York: Longman Inc.

5. Ibid., p.153.

6. Gardner, D. P. (1983, April). *A Nation at Risk: the Imperative for Educational Reform*. Retrieved July 31, 2005, from: http://www.ed.gov/pubs/NatAtRisk/index.html.

7. Lyons, N. (1998). *With Portfolio in Hand: Validating the New Teacher Professionalism*. New York: Teachers College Press.

8. Ibid.

9. Shulman, L. (1988). "The Paradox of Teacher Assessment." In S. M. Wilson (Ed.) *The Wisdom of Practice: Essays on Teaching, Learning and Learning to Teach* (p. 338). San Francisco: Jossey-Bass.

10. Payne, D. A. (2003). *Applied Educational Assessment*. Belmont, CA: Wadsworth/Thomson Learning.

3

The Teacher Portfolio
Artifact

INTRODUCTION

In Chapter 2, we mentioned two nonprofit organizations, INTASC and NBPTS, which had a pivotal role in promoting high standards for teacher preparation through performance-based assessment. NBPTS is governed by a board made up of school teachers, administrators, governors, state legislators, and business and community leaders. INTASC is a consortium of state education agencies and national education organizations whose focus is the reform of teacher certification standards. INTASC's basic premise is that "An effective teacher must be able to integrate content knowledge with the specific strengths and needs of students to assure that *all* students learn and perform at high levels."[1] INTASC standards are widely accepted as the golden yardstick that must be used by a teacher certification program to ensure that its graduates are fully prepared to become builders of a learning society. In 1992, INTASC endorsed the use of the teacher portfolio as an important standards-based, teacher-readiness assessment tool. In this chapter, we use INTASC standards as the backdrop for understanding the teacher portfolio artifact. It is critical for you to thoroughly understand what comprises an artifact. Depending on how far along you are in your teacher certification, you may have a murky or clear idea of an artifact. Finding an artifact for a standard is difficult, if not impossible, if you are not yet well versed in that standard. Before you try to find artifacts that will support a standard, you must first ask yourself whether you truly understand the meaning of the standard and are ready to show you have achieved competency in the standard. We'll see how the very process of finding artifacts for your teacher portfolio will help you get closer to your new professional role, by making you more aware of your responsibilities as a teacher.

ARTIFACTS FOR EACH STANDARD

As you may be aware, the ten INTASC standards[2] are:

1. Content Pedagogy
   The teacher understands the central concepts, tools of inquiry, and structures of the discipline(s) he or she teaches and can create learning experiences that make these aspects of subject matter meaningful for students.

2. Student Development
   The teacher understands how children learn and develop, and can provide learning opportunities that support their intellectual, social, and personal development.

3. Diverse Learners
   The teacher understands how students differ in their approaches to learning and creates instructional opportunities that are adapted to diverse learners.

4. Multiple Instructional Strategies
   The teacher understands and uses a variety of instructional strategies to encourage students' development of critical thinking, problem solving, and performance skills.

5. Motivation and Management
   The teacher uses an understanding of individual and group motivation and behavior to create a learning environment that encourages positive social interaction, active engagement in learning, and self motivation.

6. Communication and Technology
   The teacher uses knowledge of effective verbal, nonverbal, and media communication techniques to foster active inquiry, collaboration, and supportive interaction in the classroom.

7. Planning
   The teacher plans instruction based upon knowledge of subject matter, students, the community, and curriculum goals.

8. Assessment
   The teacher understands and uses formal and informal assessment strategies to evaluate and ensure the continuous intellectual, social, and physical development of the learner.

9. Reflective Practice: Professional Growth
   The teacher is a reflective practitioner who continually evaluates the effects of his or her choices and actions on others (students, parents, and other professionals in the learning community) and who actively seeks out opportunities to grow professionally.

10. School and Community Involvement
    The teacher fosters relationships with school colleagues, parents, and agencies in the larger community to support students' learning and well-being.

Is it really possible for one individual to address all of the INTASC standards without becoming a victim of serious stress and burnout? Surprisingly, the answer is yes. If you go back to thinking about your favorite teacher, you'll see that he or she was able to do just that and make it look easy. The secret is in internalizing the training you will receive in your teacher certification program, until it is second nature to you to do what the standards expect of you. Building a portfolio and selecting artifacts facilitate the process of internalization.

Artifacts are distinct elements in your teacher portfolio, such as a case study, an essay, a video clip, a recording, or any other entry that shows how proficient you are in core teaching skills, these core skills being determined by the standards followed by your institution. Artifacts can have many sources. They could be archeological (drawn from your past activities), scholastic (from courses you have taken), or be a specific program requirement related to a particular teaching standard. Some teacher programs leave it entirely up to the candidate to select artifacts for the teacher portfolio. Others lay down very specific guidelines. Regardless of the approach taken by your institution, artifacts are regarded as evidence of teaching ability. Royce Robertson, the coordinator for the teacher portfolio program at Plymouth State University, uses a class activity he calls "artifactivity" to introduce the concept of an artifact. The activity as described here is adapted from an example provided by Robertson (personal communication, October 17, 2005).

Robertson's school, like many others, uses INTASC standards as a template for their teacher portfolios. What do we mean by template? You may be familiar with templates in word-processing or presentation software programs where you can set up a look and feel that is uniform and consistent across your document. In the same sense, an institutional template would set up the colors, borders, margins, and other look and feel features that all teacher portfolios must use, and, more importantly, content-related universal requirements for all portfolios. So an INTASC standards-based teacher portfolio template would mean a portfolio containing placeholders for artifacts representing the candidate's understanding of INTASC standards. If you think of your teacher portfolio in architectural terms, the template would be the structural framework that supports it. There are a number of solid reasons for using a portfolio template, and we'll examine these in Chapter 5. Robertson is responsible for introducing the concepts of teacher portfolios and artifacts to the freshman students in their teacher education program. His introduction involves a class activity where students match artifacts to standards. Note that the activity as described here assumes a prior exposure to and understanding of the ten INTASC standards. Perhaps you will it find it useful to participate in an "artifactivity" with your classmates.

The class is divided into two groups. The first group—usually made up of about ten people—receives a set of cards, each card bearing on it one of the ten INTASC standards. This group (let's call it Group 1) is charged with discussing the meaning of the ten standards for a few minutes. At the end of the discussion, each of the ten members of the group becomes the standard bearer for one of the ten standards, and the group lines up in front of the class, each member holding up their INTASC standard.

Group 2 (made up of the rest of the students in the class) receives a set of artifact cards. Each card stands for an artifact that might be included in a teacher portfolio. The students must decide under which INTASC standard their artifact belongs. They first discuss among themselves why a given artifact would fall under a certain standard. After they have made up their minds, they take the artifact to the standard bearer in question, and must convince him or her that the artifact belongs under that standard. The standard bearer is allowed to challenge that assertion and reject the artifact if there are sufficient grounds for doing so. When all the artifacts have been accepted by the standard bearers, the standards and the artifacts are laid out on the floor in the form of a giant Jeopardy board. Both groups now join in a group discussion, and examine (a) whether any of the standards have too many artifacts, (b) whether any of the artifacts can be redistributed, and (c) what the artifacts accomplish by their inclusion in the teacher portfolio. By the end of the class, the students have a good understanding of what artifacts match each standard, and whether there can be more than one standard that fits a given artifact.

Here are some artifacts for Group 2 to match to the ten INTASC standards (listed earlier in this chapter). Note that some of these entries may not be deemed as appropriate artifacts for a teacher portfolio, depending on your institution's ground rules for teacher portfolios:

1. Résumé
2. Class observation from student teaching
3. Playing on the varsity softball team
4. A love of knitting
5. Attending a workshop on teambuilding in the classroom
6. Being CPR certified
7. Writing a paper on the development of girls in kindergarten
8. A sample individual education plan from a required course
9. A book report on *Fried Green Tomatoes,* by Fannie Flagg
10. A cookbook entry
11. A group presentation on Web development from a technology course
12. Volunteering at a group home for homeless teens
13. A lesson plan on how to teach a module on the Civil War
14. A statement of teaching philosophy
15. A multiple-choice geography test
16. Samples of student awards
17. PTA meeting minutes
18. Lesson plans from the Internet

19. Fundraising efforts for landslide victims

20. A questionnaire developed for student self-assessment

21. Examples of Web sites with interactive science quizzes

22. An audio tape of a candidate playing a musical instrument.

23. Student feedback from a class co-taught at a local elementary school

24. Reflections on classroom management

25. Work experience at a summer camp

26. Managing the day shift at Super Scoops ice cream shop in the summer

27. Writing a lesson plan on patience and persistence using Aesop's Fables' "The Tortoise and the Hare"

28. Samples of student evaluations

29. Attending a workshop on positive behavior intervention strategies

30. Participation in the student chapter of the Association of Supervision and Curriculum Development (ASCD)

31. A note sent to a parent

32. Field–day activities

33. A team–taught lesson (co-written) designed to teach basic probability using dice and coin flipping

34. A flow chart of order-processing in a fast-food restaurant

35. An outline of the process of digestion in mammals

36. Three ways to teach long division

37. A report from a field trip to the museum

38. A report of a trip to Washington, DC, with the school choir

39. Outline of plans for a summer reading program

40. Multi–age collaborative exercises in mathematics

It is also possible that an artifact may be applicable to more than one standard, depending on its use. This is another example of the contextual nature of teaching. Since there are no hard and fast rules for associating artifacts with standards, the newcomer to teaching may at first find this to be a frustrating exercise.

Consider artifact number 40, multi-age collaborative exercises in mathematics. This artifact could be used to demonstrate that the candidate measures up against INTASC standards 1 (Content Pedagogy), 2 (Student Development), and/or 4 (Multiple Instructional Strategies). The relevance of an artifact to a standard is determined by the narrative of the candidate's reflection on the artifact. Here are three hypothetical reflections accompanying artifact number 40 to support each of the three standards above. Reflection 1 reveals that the artifact is offered in support of INTASC standard 1. Reflection 2 reveals that the artifact is offered in support of INTASC standard 2. Reflection 3 reveals that the artifact is offered in support of INTASC standard 4.

Reflection 1

"I particularly enjoyed the multi-age mathematics exercise I developed for the summer mathematics workshop. This workshop was intended to allow students from grades 2 through 5 to work together on word problems, and whet their appetite for a subject (math) that has traditionally appeared in a negative and daunting light. The students met three times a week for a month during the summer vacation. Some of the older children found it empowering to serve as guides for the younger ones. I instructed the 'guides' not to provide leading questions or answers but to lead their 'protégé' into discovering the solution as well as finding ways to get to the solution. It soon became apparent to me that all children possess the ability to develop the numerical and logical skills needed for solving word problems. We worked more on breaking down the problem to manageable chunks and less on the solution itself. The concept of multiplication can be understood by students in grade 2 provided they have already mastered counting and grid development exercises. This helped students overcome their fear of math. I feel this artifact could apply equally to INTASC standard 1 or 2 but offer it in support of standard 1."

Reflection 2

"The multi-age collaborative mathematics exercise was one I found particularly instructive for me as a teacher. As the middle sibling in a family of five children, I remember accompanying my elder sisters to the candy store and watching them buy candy while Mom and Dad watched from a few feet away without becoming involved. I also learned how a pack of 18 sweets can be divided among five children (and why it was acceptable for the older children to get more!). I used the theme of a visit to the candy store in this class. I was excited to affirm that learning occurs not just in the classroom but also in social situations, in small and large diverse groups. Just as, as a child, I learned how to make change for a dollar as well as experience team dynamics, the students in this class had learning experiences on more than one level—personal, social, and intellectual. I believe this artifact supports my understanding of INTASC standard 2."

Reflection 3

"I offer this artifact as an example of INTASC standard 4. I divided the class into several small groups composed of older and younger students. All the groups had access to a variety of tools and strategies for solving the word problems presented to them, such as whiteboards, pens, paper, modeling clay, beads, abacus, and grids. It was interesting to see that regardless of age, many of these tools were used in different ways by each group. While it is true that some of the older children showed more skill in breaking down the problem into sub-problems, it was clear that even among students with a similar level of preparation, having a variety of strategies for problem-solving was very important since each student brings his or her own unique perspective to the classroom."

THE SELF-INQUIRY PROCESS

There's a reason why no manual on building portfolios can give you a formula to use for selecting artifacts. There is no single perfect artifact for a given standard because so much depends on context. Building a teacher portfolio is a distinctly individual activity, like teaching. You'll find that the strategies and exercises in this chapter lead you to experience firsthand why your teaching and your teacher portfolio are so inextricably tied. I cannot overemphasize the fact that you will have to translate the suggestions and directions on portfolio building to your unique situation and the needs of your program. The quality of your portfolio will be determined by your efforts and dedication in bringing it all together. That being said, how does a candidate find the most appropriate artifact?

A great artifact is one that speaks to your ability, sincerity, and passion for teaching. To fit his or her unique situation, a candidate must use a process of self-inquiry to select artifacts. A standardized "one size fits all" approach to portfolio building must be replaced by an emphasis on self-inquiry. Let's consider why.

Process versus Product

If you ever move out of state, you may have to pass a written driver's test based on the new state's road rules. You could apply yourself to memorizing the rules and regulations in the driver's manual with a view to passing the test. If, however, you apply yourself to studying the manual because becoming intimately familiar with the rules could be instrumental in saving your life, you would probably become a better driver and incidentally pass the test. The first step for portfolio building is to desist from viewing the portfolio merely as a requirement for certification. Your portfolio is not something to "take care of" or "get out of the way." For the passionate teacher, it's a way of life.

Construction versus Compilation

At first you may be tempted to amass vast amounts of material, such as papers you wrote, certificates you received, accounts of your hobbies and activities, and anything else you believe you can remotely associate with your teaching abilities. You may have a fear that you do not have enough material to offer as artifacts for your teacher portfolio. As a beginning teacher or a recent candidate for teacher certification, this fear is certainly justified. However, the desire to "save everything" could get in the way of producing a great portfolio, because volume obfuscates relevance. It would be a good idea to keep your focus on quality, excellence, and relevance right from the outset.

Start by considering, for each standard that you must exemplify, what kind of supportive evidence would be appropriate and within your ability to provide. Next, work toward getting that evidence together in the form of one or more artifacts. There may be some artifacts that are predetermined by your program, such as papers from certain coursework. In the case of these artifacts, the time saved in finding or selecting the artifact can be spent on revising and refining it. View each artifact as your personal spokesperson. In your absence, your artifact should represent you and the continually evolving dimensions of your teaching and learning. This emphasis on quality over quantity will transform portfolio building from a chore into an activity that energizes and grows you.

Communication versus Defense

Most programs will require you to write a reflection on each artifact, offering reasons why you selected this item as an artifact, and why you chose it as evidence for a particular standard. Try to offer this rationale as if it were part of a dialogue with yourself or your reviewer, rather than merely stating a string of reasons. A "communicative" approach will involve examples and discussions that provoke thought and further reflection, and engender the construction of knowledge. On the other hand, a mere statement of rationale will sound forced or stilted and induce fatigue in you and your reviewer.

Interpretation versus Imitation

When you first begin work on your portfolio, it may be tempting to build your artifacts in a formulaic manner. You may feel that the safest course is to follow a pattern of analysis used by someone who has already successfully built a portfolio. There are two flaws to this reasoning that are not always obvious. First, your experiences are your own, and you will find it hard to fit them to someone else's mind maps. What appears to be the easier route becomes an exercise in frustration. Second, you may unwittingly produce an artifact that looks plagiarized. Study the examples provided to you as a means of understanding the concept of an artifact, and then apply the concept in your own unique way.

Believe in the power of your own mind to interpret and analyze ideas, take sides, re-evaluate your stand, and forge new directions. You need not feel compelled to make your portfolio or the artifacts in it fit anyone's mold. The uniqueness of your portfolio will make it shine. Take time to reflect on your beliefs about teaching, and be prepared to show that your ideas are consistent. Be a risk taker. Share and celebrate your most inspired moments as well as the times when your plans did not quite pan out. In doing this, you will be helped by the variety of multimedia opportunities available today.

QUESTIONS TO ASK ABOUT STANDARDS
AND ARTIFACTS

What is this process of self-inquiry that will help you select meaningful artifacts? It is made up of a set of questions for you to ask before, during, and after the process of selecting artifacts. You can practice this approach with one or more friends, a family member, or by yourself. With time, the process will become second nature to you. It will be clear to you that some of the questions in this inquiry are critical to the arti-fact, while others are helpful in short-listing potential artifacts for a given standard.

Before selecting artifacts, start by asking the following questions:

1. Do I understand and fulfill the standard? If so, how do I fulfill the standard?

    If you are unsure how you meet a particular standard, you are not ready to start the process of selecting an artifact for it. Defer this activity unless you are sure you have mastered the skills necessary to meet this standard.

2. How can I most effectively express how I fulfill the standard?

    There are innumerable ways to demonstrate your fulfillment of a particular standard, drawing examples from a multitude of media, including narratives of classroom experiences, lesson plans, research papers, studies, projects, conversations, extracurricular activities, and observations of your teaching. Based on your individual situation, you will find one that is appropriate.

3. Do I have relevant feedback from my students, peers, or supervisors that pertains to this standard?

    In most cases, providing alternative perspectives can be more effective than just merely giving your own viewpoint. Some artifacts lend themselves more easily to this. For example, a recorded conversation between you and your students in which you discuss an assignment can reveal more about your teaching than a narrative in which you make all the observations and readings of participants' handling of the assignment.

4. Have I participated in any activities that directly pertain to this standard?

    You may have had opportunities to participate in a study on a topic related to a standard, thus getting more than the usual exposure to activities related to the standard. By all means, use these opportunities by finding artifacts related to them.

5. In what way was I rewarded for my participation in these activities?

    Artifacts that inherently reveal how much you benefited from an experience are more likely to convey your fulfillment of a standard than are artifacts that simply describe the experience. Your reward from an activity could be the joy you got out of the successful outcome of the activity, or recognition you received for a job well done.

6. Do I have any milestones to report in this area?

    You may have made greater strides in one area than in another. Find artifacts that convey the purpose of the artifact, and show how they represent the accomplishment of an important milestone.

7. What significant experiences can I recall that are pertinent to this standard?

    The more practice you have had in a particular area of your teaching preparation, the more experiences you will have available to draw from and use as artifacts. It stands to reason that the areas you have mastered will be the areas where you find your best artifacts.

8. Is this standard an area of strength, weakness, or development for me?

    While you and your supervisors will strive to prepare you in every core area of teaching ability, there will always be a few areas in which you do better than others. Your reflections on each artifact must include an understanding of your current strengths, weaknesses, and areas of development. Use your artifacts to show that you have a clear understanding of where you need to develop more, where you feel the strongest, and where you have gaps in your preparation. Toward the end of your teacher education program, you may be able to effectively compare two artifacts for a given standard— one taken from an experience early in the program and the other more recent, showing how much you have learned.

9. What kind of media would be most effective in an artifact for this standard?

If you are using electronic portfolio software, you will be able to include virtually all kinds of multimedia, such as artifacts from audio, video, and graphical applications. Be selective about the media and make sure it is relevant and useful for the given standard supported by the artifact in that media.

10. Are there any specific requirements for artifacts for this standard?

If you have been provided with ground rules or guidelines for artifacts for a given standard, be sure to include these in your evaluation of the artifact.

After selecting potential artifacts, subject each artifact to the following questions:

1. Does the artifact speak for itself?
2. Would it be easy to make a case for using this artifact for this standard?
3. Does this artifact fit this standard better than it fits any other standard?
4. Does this artifact support more than one standard?
5. Do I feel comfortable sharing the artifact?
6. Does this artifact have value outside of the portfolio?
7. Is this artifact "the best I could come up with" or the best example of this standard as exemplified in my work?
8. Will this be the only artifact I offer for this standard?
9. What do I like most about this artifact?
10. Does the artifact manifest my passion for teaching?

APPLYING THE SELF-INQUIRY PROCESS

Let's try to apply the self-inquiry process to INTASC standard 1.

INTASC Standard 1: Content Pedagogy

"The teacher understands the central concepts, tools of inquiry, and structures of the discipline(s) he or she teaches and can create learning experiences that make these aspects of subject matter meaningful for students."

Self-Inquiry: *Do I understand and fulfill the standard? If yes, how do I fulfill the standard?*

There are two parts to this standard. The first part pertains to your knowledge of the subjects you will be teaching and implies a solid grasp of the key concepts and methods of the subject, along with a continual effort on your part to stay abreast of advances in the field. Your program will have numerous ways to assess your subject knowledge at a given point in time using a variety of assessment methods, such as written or multiple-choice exams, interviews, or presentations. How will you ensure that you continue to build on this knowledge? The second part refers to your ability to translate your deep knowledge into ideas to which your students can relate and turn into a part of their individual knowledge nexus.

Before you can compile a list of artifacts to consider as evidence of standard 1, you must be sure you understand the ramifications of both parts of the standard. Let us examine the meaning and implications of this standard together.

Keeping Up with Expanding Subject Knowledge

While the Internet has made access to certain resources easier, the information overload that accompanies it can easily dilute the depth of learning and teaching of a given subject. To stay current in her field, the teacher must be prepared to spend many hours outside of her preparation and teaching time reading books and journals from her subject area, talking to experts, and attending seminars and workshops. She must fearlessly plunge into unfamiliar activities, including those involving hands-on experience with the use of technology. In a nutshell, the teacher must first and foremost be a learner.

Another characteristic of our current educational milieu is the development of interdisciplinary studies. We finally see that it is hard to comprehend anything from the perspective of a single discipline. Knowledge involves awareness of a variety of complementary perspectives of reality. A teacher who cannot think in multiple disciplines will soon feel way out of her depth. For example, if you look at the field of artificial intelligence (AI), you'll see that it raises many thought-provoking questions such as "Is the mind identical with the brain?" Answers to such questions intersect subjects such as brain chemistry, computer science, philosophy, and ethics.

There's another important unstated implication of the standard of content pedagogy. To be successful, the teacher must become comfortable with the idea that she is not always the most knowledgeable person in the classroom. Back in the day, the village schoolmaster held the exalted position of being a repository of knowledge, but things have changed given the free access we have to research, world news, and economic changes. A big difference between novices and experienced teachers is in the teacher's comfort level with classroom management. The newbie teacher enters the classroom fully intending to keep a tight control over it. The more experienced teacher is able to let go, and does not feel threatened by an overzealous or hyperactive student who gets everything right the first time.

Artifact Hint: *Look for artifacts that a) demonstrate how you are a lifelong learner and b) showcase your research or studies.*

Conveying Ideas to Your Students

When a teacher enters the classroom to meet her new students, she has little or no previous knowledge of the background or level of preparedness of each of her wards. Before she can begin to create a meaningful learning situation for each child, she needs to get to know them as individuals. Even if she cannot capture a detailed unique blueprint of each child's learning framework, she will need to gain some familiarity with the student's background and make educated guesses about some areas of this blueprint. She'll also have to provide for a way of constantly getting feedback on how each individual student is handling the continuous stream of new information, and how the information is being turned into knowledge. This will help her fine-tune her grasp of the student's preparation level, reducing the guesswork and enabling her to continue creating learning experiences that match the child's needs. If you were that new teacher, how would you go about gathering these learning blueprints for each child in your care, given that you have to divide your time among twenty-five students, have a limited amount of preparation time, and need every minute you have in the classroom to cover the required curriculum? Your own background, training, and teaching philosophy will determine how you answer this question.

It would not be an exaggeration to state that we live in a digital universe. A large number of us are connected to a network twenty-four hours a day, seven days a week. Here are more than twenty different uses of a digital network, all of which are now commonplace: waking up to a radio alarm; watching the headlines, the weather, and the traffic report on television; stopping to buy gas at the corner gas station and using a credit card to pay for it at the pump; navigating traffic lights using a networked infrastructure, including cruise cards through toll booths; a GPS as standard equipment on your SUV; the ubiquitous cell phone being used for phone calls, text messaging, and checking on stock prices; company intranet usage as well as chat program usage; elementary school children researching a topic on the Internet; Internet banking and shopping; registering for and taking courses and checking grades on-line; gaming; browsing library catalogs; downloading software; checking email; booking vacations over the Internet; surfing real estate; finding a telephone number; and paying taxes.

Children today are more comfortable with this digital universe than are the adults in their environment because of getting oriented to it at a very early age. By the time a child has reached school-going age, he or she is already being bombarded by multimedia. His or her brain is accustomed to processing a large amount of diverse information. Children as young as six years may know that there are American soldiers fighting a war in Iraq, and that a really big wave called a tsunami killed thousands of people on the other side of the globe. However, they are far from ready to digest all the information to which they have access. How each individual child reacts to these stimuli depends on factors such as where they live, the extent of the child's immediate family's involvement with these inputs, and the kind of stimuli they receive.

Your challenge is to teach a class in such a way that each student a) gets interested in what you have to say (through the hooks you provide), b) is able to relate to the concept you are presenting, and c) discovers one or more bridges that connect what they already know to what you want then to understand. Assuming you know your subject so well that you have a mind-map of the underlying conceptual architecture, you can distinguish between ideas that are basic and foundational, those that are intermediate steps in the conceptual ladder, and those ideas that are additional, interesting notions that could embellish the teaching of a concept but are not essential to it. Armed with this mental map, and a general idea of the background of the students in your class, you are able to plan your lesson and successfully teach each segment of your curriculum.

Artifact Hint: *Look for artifacts that illustrate how you are able to build conceptual bridges for students.*

Self-Inquiry: *How can I most effectively express how I fulfill the standard?*

After brainstorming and reflecting on various possibilities, you decide that you will use as artifacts for this standard the following elements: a lesson plan, a narrative about the lesson including examples of student participation and feedback (taken from your class notes), and a simple graph of student performance on an informal test on the topic, administered after the unit was completed. Together these elements would combine teacher and student perspectives and give a contextual example of your content pedagogy. In your reflection, you will refer to these elements and bring them together as evidence for the standard. Include a write-up that shows your grasp of the standard, with several examples and illustrations.

The following might be your artifacts:

Lesson plan: You decide to adapt a lesson plan from the *National Geographic* site to teach about Egypt.[3]

Class notes, including student feedback: "The lesson plan I used for the unit on Egypt was a success. Students watched with great interest as I showed the clips from the museum's archives on the process of mummification. Some of the questions I asked about climate in the Sahara elicited responses that showed me that the students were making connections between cultural practices and climate. For example, one student asked 'Would they have had mummies if Egypt was a very cold place like Antarctica?' One of the students talked about the Egypt exhibit at the museum she had visited with her family last summer. My introductory segment set the stage for the discussions and explanations that followed. (For example, to teach about the mummification process, I first discussed how various things decay under different conditions.)"

Informal test results summarized: "18 out of 20 students were able to answer the questions on the segment with over 85 percent accuracy."

Reflection: "This lesson plan was successful because it was able to capture student attention right from the outset. It also had a good logical sequence of topics and underlying concepts. For example, if I had not discussed decay and climate before discussing mummification, the results may not have been as good. The survey on Egypt I handed out last week revealed to me that very few students had been exposed to information on Egypt prior to this unit. This knowledge helped me adapt the *National Geographic* lesson plan to suit my class's needs. Instead of the computer segment, I used film clips that the whole class could watch together. This avoided the problem of differing computer abilities as well as the problem of not having an adequate number of terminals with Internet access."

INTASC Standard 2: Student Development

"The teacher understands how children learn and develop, and can provide learning opportunities that support their intellectual, social, and personal development."

Self-Inquiry: *Do I understand and fulfill the standard? If yes, how do I fulfill the standard?*

Once again, let us discuss this standard together. You may choose to analyze and discuss the other standards on your own in a similar way, at the start of your inquiry into the standard.

Childhood and developmental studies are a required part of a teacher certification program, and you are no doubt taking courses in this area. Since the paper *Nation at Risk* was published, an even greater responsibility has been placed on the teacher. Your support of the students' development is expected to span much more than just intellectual accomplishments. You are responsible for guiding your students' social and personal development as well. Let's pause to consider how our changing perceptions of the teaching and learning process may have resulted in enlarging the teacher's role.

We now have greater awareness of different cultural approaches to teaching, the age at which school should begin, and the content of the curriculum for different grades. The same factors that make children more technologically savvy at an early age lead to their immersion in a highly interactive world. The world is shrinking. For example, before email became a household word, it might have taken months for a child to interact with a pen pal in another country. Today, two children geographically separated by thousands of miles of open water can communicate as if they are in the same room, thanks to modern technology. There's a sense of urgency for people to be able to reach out and understand each other. The growing involvement between parents and teachers through PTAs, and the popularity of community programs forging these bonds, is another case in point. To be a successful participant in this world, the child needs guidance in social interaction skills. At the same time, the child also needs to develop responsibility as an individual and a sense of his or her uniqueness. The epals.com[4] site provides great examples of a child's intellectual, social, and personal development needs and the teacher's involvement in providing for these needs. Here's a school from Thailand looking for a partner school in another country:[5]

"My class is a mattayom 1 (grade 7) class of 30 students. We would like to make friends with ePals around the world to practice our English skills and learn about different places. My students are very excited about starting this project. We can write about Thailand and our lives here and would like to learn about different places."

ePals is also a channel for student-safe email and collaborative international classroom exchange. For instance, a third grade student in China can interact collaboratively with his third grade counterpart in the United States. Teachers can collaborate as well. Discussion boards for different age groups are available with mediated exchanges. Email channels for parents, children, and teachers are another feature of this exchange site. Opportunities for shared projects, cross-cultural dialogues, and language learning traverse a wide variety of curriculum areas, including language arts, technology, geography, history, civics, community and government, citizenship education, science, health, and social studies.

However, even where access to technology is limited, there are many ways in which a teacher can celebrate the cultural and linguistic diversity of today's classroom using valuable traditional approaches such as painting, drama, story-telling, and literature. As a teacher, you will be expected to provide, nurture, and participate in such opportunities for student development. You will also be expected to develop strong relationships with your peers, parents, and the community at large. They will provide excellent resources to help you fill this important teacher responsibility.

Artifact Hint: *Look for artifacts that reveal there are many dimensions to student development.*

Self-Inquiry: *How can I most effectively express how I fulfill the standard?*

You and your students were recently involved with the community in a fund-raising activity to support local firefighters. You decide to use artifacts from this project to support INTASC standard 2. Your set includes the following elements: a) a narrative describing the project and why your students got involved with it, b) photographs of students working with the community, c) student narratives about the project explaining the strategy and objectives, and d) a spreadsheet showing the balance sheet from the project, prepared by the student project leader.

Applying the self-inquiry process helped you find suitable artifacts for this standard. For example:

Do I have relevant feedback from my students, peers, or supervisors that pertains to this standard?

Have I participated in any activities that directly pertain to this standard?

Your artifact set for this standard reveals that student development is not restricted to the classroom. The project you share with the reviewer shows that students' intellectual, social, and personal development were addressed. Among many other things, they learned about the arduous work of firefighting, the value of teamwork, the elements of planning, accounting, and project management, and the value of working with the community. Your artifact set includes student perspectives as well as yours. (If possible, you could also include statements from parents, peers, and members of the firefighter organization that was served by the project.) The project was a relevant activity and well worth reporting.

In what way was I rewarded for my participation in these activities?

Reflection: "The firefighter's fundraiser raised not just money but all of our spirits! I was very impressed by the students' dedication to this effort. They spent many long hours in planning and performing the work that was required, even though this meant sacrificing many of their weekends and leisure activities. This was a joint project co-chaired by the accounting, social studies, and physical education teachers. We feel that the project "grew" our students on many levels as they coped with very adult responsibilities and worked to fulfill them. I am truly proud of what they have accomplished!"

What kind of media would be most effective in an artifact for this standard?

This artifact set used four kinds of media: written narrative, recordings of participant comments, photographs, and spreadsheets.

Are there any specific requirements for artifacts for this standard?

This artifact met the ground rules provided for the portfolio process.

INTASC Standard 9: Reflective Practice: Professional Growth

"The teacher is a reflective practitioner who continually evaluates the effects of his or her choices and actions on others (students, parents, and other professionals in the learning community) and who actively seeks out opportunities to grow professionally."

Apply the self-inquiry process to discover whether you are ready to address this standard, and then consider what evidence you might offer.

Artifact Hint: *Look for artifacts to highlight actions and activities in your everyday teaching practice that demonstrate your commitment to professional growth.*

You decide to use an artifact set of three different but related items as evidence for this standard. The first is a reflection on a student named Joey in the grade 7 writing class you co-taught with your mentor. Your mentor has informed you that Joey has ADHD (attention deficit hyperactivity disorder). This is your first experience working with an ADHD child. Around the same time, you also attended a workshop on learners who are gifted and talented. You decide to include a reflection from what you learned in that workshop. The third item in your artifact set is a set of discussions with your mentor about Joey's needs and accomplishments. Your mentor is not only familiar with Joey, but is also an experienced elementary and middle school teacher. These discussions span a period of three months, starting from your first encounter with the children in Joey's class through the end of that practicum period. Together these items form a supporting triangle demonstrating your professional growth. To bring these items together into one meaningful braid, you write a reflection that describes your journey from being someone unfamiliar with the needs and traits of children with ADHD and children who are gifted, to someone who now sees that these categories or characterizations of learners are not isolated but often overlap.

Reflection: "When I first met Joey's class I knew I was in for a challenging classroom management experience. Along with my mentor, I had gone over some background information on each student. I had reviewed previous work on tests and assignments, and read notes from assessments that indicated for each student where his or her strengths and weaknesses lay. I had done my homework on the needs learners with ADHD, and knowing that ADHD was not treated as a discrete disability, I was prepared to provide multiple opportunities for successful learning for students such as Joey within the regular classroom environment. One of the first exercises we handed out to the class was a short writing assignment based on a story we had read the previous day, to be completed at home. The class had learned several new vocabulary words, and was asked to use as many of these words as possible in the writing assignment."

"When I read Joey's essay, the level of writing appeared to be at least three grades higher than expected, and frankly, my first thought was that Joey had received help from an older sibling on his homework, or worse yet, had had his homework done by someone older. Surely, a child who seemed unable to focus for even a few minutes at a time in the classroom could not have managed to write an essay of this caliber, containing all the covered vocabulary words, and several new ones. In my mind, if a student was diagnosed as ADHD, he or she could not at the same time be a learner with giftedness. My interactions with Joey, my participation in the Gifted Learners workshop, and the conversations I had with my co-teacher and mentor were responsible for the transformations in my own understanding of the needs and abilities of learners falling under either the ADHD and/or the Gifted characterization."

"I was able to see that a learner who needed more time than the average to complete an assignment, clear and concise directions on completing the assignment, and assistance with staying on task could at the same time be a highly verbal and abstract thinker, who could nicely tie together ideas and concepts that might prove hard for the average student to assimilate. At first I found this to be a startling and contradictory idea, but listening to the speakers in the Gifted Learners workshop redefined my understanding of learning abilities in general. It also helped to have an exposure to Gardner's writings on multiple intelligences. Conversations with my mentor helped solidify this understanding in my mind, and allowed me to see students such as Joey in a new light. The experience was also instructive in letting me realize that I must guard against 'judging' learners based on theories I have accepted without adequate questioning or reflection."

INTASC Standard 10: School and Community Involvement

"The teacher fosters relationships with school colleagues, parents, and agencies in the larger community to support students' learning and well-being."

Perhaps you can see that the artifact set submitted for INTASC standard 2 could also have served the purpose of INTASC standard 10. The decision to use it for one or the other or both is a decision that will need to made by the candidate on a case-by-case basis, assuming your program allows you to use the same artifact for more than one standard. When you have numerous competing artifacts, or have one artifact that could serve multiple standards, using the post-selection, self-inquiry questions will help you decide which way to go:

Does the artifact speak for itself?

Would it be easy to make a case for using this artifact for this standard?

Does this artifact fit this standard better than it fits any other standard?

Does this artifact support more than one standard?

Is this artifact "the best I could come up with" or the best example of this standard as exemplified in my work?

Will this be the only artifact I offer for this standard?

What do I like most about this artifact?

Does the artifact manifest my passion for teaching?

Here's a reflection that might have been written after you decided to use the Firefighter Fundraiser artifact set to support both INTASC standard 10 and INTASC standard 2:

Reflection: "Research in cognitive science (interdisciplinary studies of the human mind) has revealed that are connections between levels of learning (motor, physical, etc.), and the way one learns different subjects, facts, and concepts. This has led to a better understanding of learning as a whole and how advanced levels of learning can be achieved. The meaning of the term 'intelligence' has undergone radical transformations as a consequence of these interdisciplinary studies. In his book on the theory of multiple intelligences, Howard Gardner states: 'My review of earlier studies of intelligence and cognition has suggested the existence of a number of different intellectual strengths, or competencies, each of which may have its own developmental history.'[6]

"We can see that these advances help dismiss the old idea that one is born 'stupid' or 'smart.' Gardner also said: 'While we may continue to use the words smart and stupid, and while IQ tests may persist for certain purposes, the monopoly of those who believe in a single general intelligence has come to an end.'[7] A teacher is committed to nurturing each child's unique strengths—whether it has to do with numbers, colors, or musical notes, or some other realm of understanding. Getting the students involved in a community activity not only helps them develop on many fronts, it also gives students a variety of ways in which they can find success and develop confidence and self-esteem."

Use the above process of reflective self-inquiry to find artifacts for each area of your portfolio. As you can see, an artifact can be a stand-alone item such as a paper on a subject, or a set of artifacts that together support a standard, as in the examples above.

Today's teachers must be comfortable with change, and the fact that they do not know everything. To build real expertise, the teacher must be skillful in picking out what is vital to convey on a topic, before other concepts dependent on the framework of ideas related to this topic can be absorbed. A teacher may have a wealth of resources available to her to use in her teaching, such as teaching ideas, lesson plans, and multimedia resources. She can't expect to just blindly apply these resources in her classroom. Rather, she must be selective and adaptive by carefully choosing the examples and methods that will work for the students with whose learning she is charged. She must be well-versed in her subject area, but beyond that, possess true expertise in teaching—the ability to customize resources for her purposes, and convey a solid core of ideas. A learning society needs members who are informed, discriminating, excited about learning, and able to make connections between ideas they have learned about in different contexts. I hope you can see that the portfolio process parallels what is asked of you as a teacher.

SUMMARY

The Internet Age has changed the participants and the conditions under which teaching and learning take place. Various standards bodies have raised the bar for teacher certification by spelling out what's expected of teachers. Through reflection and practice, a teacher can internalize these standards and develop his or her professionalism. The portfolio process facilitates this transformation through the reflective act of choosing artifacts for the teacher portfolio, while offering the candidate a chance to be involved in his or her own assessment.

The portfolio owner can learn his or her own strengths and areas for improvement as a teacher in ongoing, context-rich, personal, and professional growth opportunities. The teaching profession as a whole benefits in several ways: the availability of a broader range of evidence of teaching competencies than is offered by exit exams alone[8]; a sense of community; the opportunity to see strengths and weaknesses in the accreditation process[9]; and a way to make the concept of teacher accountability a meaningful and practical idea.[10]

Here are some ideas for artifacts. Which ones do you think are particularly meaningful for a teacher portfolio? Why? Write reflections on the artifacts that you selected. At the end of the list, add other ideas for artifacts that you think are appropriate for pre-service or in-service teacher portfolios.

- Recorded class discussion on capital punishment
- Recorded conversations with two different students on their understanding of a math problem
- A suggested model for grading group projects explaining participation ground rules
- Research paper on early childhood learning
- An essay on your memories of your favorite subject when you were in grade school
- A position paper on whether parents should be involved in students' homework in elementary, middle, and high school
- Your reflections on what the government can do to improve teaching standards
- A video of a speech by a community leader you admire
- A video of your students participating in a competition
- Samples or snippets from a community activity in which you were involved
- Award criteria for an award you won

- Samples of artwork you created or a group effort to which you contributed
- Your ideas for curbing the drug problem in schools
- A narrative about a historical film and a critique of it
- Ideas for interdisciplinary activities drawn from two fields you particularly enjoy, and how you would use these ideas in your classroom
- A paper or a recording of a class discussion discussing how the Internet Age has changed the nature of teaching and learning

ENDNOTES

1. Retrieved September 3, 2005, from http://www.ccsso.org/projects/ Interstate_New_Teacher_Assessment_and_Support_Consortium/#Mission.
2. INTASC. (1992). *Model Standards for Beginning Teacher Licensing, Assessment and Development: A Resource for State Dialogue*. Retrieved October 9, 2005, from http:// www.ccsso.org/content/pdfs/corestrd.pdf.
3. Retrieved February 19, 2006, from http://www.nationalgeographic.com/ xpeditions/lessons/17/g35/desert.html.
4. Retrieved September 3, 2005, from http://www.epals.com.
5. Retrieved September 4, 2005, from http://www.epals.com/esearch/ ?st=bs&cou=th.
6. Gardner, H. (1983). *Frames of Mind: The Theory of Multiple Intelligences*. New York, NY: Basic Books.
7. Gardner, H. (1999). *Intelligence Reframed: Multiple Intelligences for the 21st Century*. New York, NY: Basic Books.
8. Cambridge, B. L. (2001). "Electronic Portfolios as Knowledge Builders." *Electronic Portfolios: Emerging Practices in Student, Faculty and Institutional Learning*. Washington, DC: American Association for Higher Education.
9. Sickle, M. V., Bogan, M. B., Kamen, B., Baird, W., and Butcher, C. (2005). "Dilemmas faced establishing portfolio assessment of pre-service teachers in the Southeastern United States." *College Student Journal*. Retrieved October 10, 2005, from http://infotrac-college.thomsonlearning.com.
10. Kayler, M. A. (2004). "Portfolio Assessment and Teacher Development." *Academic Exchange Quarterly*. Retrieved November 9, 2005, from http://infotrac-college.thomsonlearning.com.

4

Building Your Teacher Portfolio

INTRODUCTION

We saw how the teacher portfolio has the potential to help you internalize the core requirements of a teacher education program and grow as a professional. Now that you have a better understanding of the teacher portfolio artifact, you are ready to move on to the next steps in the process of creating your very own teacher portfolio. To keep things simple, we'll assume that you are just getting started with the portfolio process. However, this chapter and the next will be beneficial even if you have already started gathering artifacts. Creating your teacher portfolio is an iterative process and you'll make many passes, swaps, and revisions to bring it all together. Since artifacts are the core of your portfolio, we'll continue to discuss artifacts as we move along.

We have said that your teacher portfolio records the milestones of your professional journey. However, these milestones don't necessarily correspond to a particular level in your program or the completion of a requirement. The milestone could be an "Aha!" moment in a class you're co-teaching when a particular teaching strategy proves very successful, or conversely, a lesson you learned the hard way. It could be a discovery you make about yourself as a teacher after a conversation with a peer or mentor. Include examples of what you consider your strongest (and weakest) teaching moments. As you get engaged in the portfolio process, you'll probably begin to see the portfolio less as a form of assessment and more as an opportunity for you to grow. "We cannot encourage our students to engage in a transformative process if we are unwilling to do so ourselves."[1]

The teacher education program in which you are enrolled may be more or less formalized. It may use a template based on INTASC standards such as the one we examined in Chapter 3, use a different template, or perhaps no template at all. Your school may be using paper portfolios, portfolios in digital format on a

CD or Web page, or an electronic portfolio software program. (We'll look at electronic portfolio software in Chapter 6). From the discussion on standards and artifacts, you now understand what kind of artifacts you might include as evidence of your fulfillment of teacher certification standards. For a teacher education program using the INTASC standards as a template, the teacher portfolio would have several sections, including one for each of the ten INTASC standards. Each of those sections would be a container for the artifacts selected as evidence of the teacher competency in question. Other teacher education programs require similar artifacts (artifacts representing the same universally accepted teacher competencies), but allow the teacher candidates to use their discretion and creativity to organize the sections of the portfolio.

Regardless of matters of format or structure, the portfolio will still need to show that a) you have an excellent grasp of your subject area and know how to teach it, b) you have a well-considered teaching philosophy that is revealed in your artifacts, c) you are able to articulate the reasons for your choice of approaches and methods in each teaching situation, and d) you are a continual learner. Your reviewers will want to know you as an individual with particular characteristics, interests, experiences, teaching goals, strategies, and pedagogical preferences. You might add other artifacts that *you* deem valuable in painting a picture of yourself as a teacher. Your portfolio should convey all this in a format that will be captivating and informative, without being overwhelming.

We can safely assume that a generic listing of portfolio sections that would be applicable to either approach would contain several of the entries in Table 4.1:

When teacher portfolios first emerged, they were an attempt to stimulate the process of reflection in the novice teacher by capturing a slice of a classroom activity or assignment that was particularly meaningful to the student teacher. The student teacher's reflections would be a starting point for a deeper, more long-term exploration into what really constituted his or her teaching philosophy. Samples of students' completed assignments, a description of the objectives of the assignment or activity, student interview snippets, and a description of how the activity had been conducted by the student teacher would together provide a context within which the teacher's acts could be understood. It was of course easier for the candidate to offer "congratulatory" artifacts articulating his or her accomplishments in an activity done well. However, educators supporting the portfolio process wanted to include accounts of bad days in the classroom as much as the great ones, as both offered learning opportunities to the novice. Both were needed to set the stage for him or her to develop a sense of identity as a teacher—an identity they would share with other teaching professionals, but one that would bear their own unique stamp. Other early artifacts included a statement of the goals of the teaching program voiced by the student teacher, and a reflective commentary by both the observing teacher-mentor as well as themselves on the extent to which they believed these goals had been accomplished. There was a lot more emphasis on including résumé-like entries on the one hand and free-form journal entries on the other. While both of these are valuable and still used in teacher portfolios, you will see that they paved

TABLE 4.1

- Introduction
- Program goals and expected outcomes
- Candidate's mission
- Personal profile
- Prior training
- Relevant work experience
- Awards and other accomplishments pertinent to teaching
- Evidence of work done in each content area such as mathematics, writing, cultural studies, and science
- One or more teaching samples including lesson plans, class and home work, and a debrief session after the class
- Candidate's students' work, graded and ungraded
- Sample student projects devised by the candidate
- Recorded discussions with supervisors and mentors on teaching approaches and the context in which each one might be employed
- Observations and feedback from one or more class observers
- Reflective self-assessments of one's own teaching
- One or more case studies of candidate's students
- Papers and presentations from various courses forming the core of the teacher education program
- Classroom management strategies
- Student feedback and references
- Candidate's response to student feedback where applicable
- An explanation of standards, benchmarks, and rubrics (a method for assigning scores along with an explanation of the criteria used for scoring) used in the evaluation of the teacher portfolio
- A statement of the candidate's teaching philosophy
- Concluding notes

the way for less linear, more in-depth presentations of the candidate's accomplishments through deep, guided reflections, recordings of conversations, and continuing, long-term dialogues on relevant topics.

Each artifact that is selected to go into the teacher portfolio must be consciously chosen, offer contextual evidence, and serve a specific purpose. Ask yourself two questions about each artifact you want to include, making sure you say yes to at least one of the questions:

- Does this artifact reveal my understanding of an important teaching standard?
- Does it offer a contextual illustration of my unique approach?

Selecting the entries that will constitute these artifacts, arranging them, and linking them are part of an active, participative process that will help crystallize an image of the teacher you are. By providing your supervisors with a way to assess your teaching abilities within a meaningful context, your teacher portfolio will effectively supplement other forms of assessment that may be in place in your program.

Some of the entries in Table 4.1 are straightforward, for example, a write-up about program goals and expected outcomes, papers and presentations from various courses, and explanations of standards, benchmarks, and rubrics used by the program. You can get some of these from your institution. There are some that constitute the heart of your portfolio, particularly those that involve deep reflection and feedback. The artifacts that you select for these areas must uniquely represent you and what you bring to the act of teaching. However, the portfolio you build is greater than the sum of its artifacts. Let's explore the nuances of the portfolio process.

THE THREE PHASES OF BUILDING A PORTFOLIO

The difference between building a portfolio that helps you grow as a professional and merely compiling a folder of artifacts lies in the process. The process of building your teacher portfolio is defined by three distinct phases: the introspective phase, the design phase, and the implementation phase. The introspective phase will dominate some parts of your portfolio more than others. This is where the sincerity and passion you feel about your work manifests itself. In the design phase, you choose the artifact(s) that will lend credence to your skills and mesh with your pedagogy. Finally, in the implementation phase, you connect the artifacts with one another following the direction you set in the introspective and design phases. Allow your creativity to shine in each of the three phases, and your well-constructed portfolio will speak for itself. The teacher portfolio you build may be used as an assessment tool, but it is not an end in itself. It is a vehicle to take you from your candidacy to your teaching self, over a long but exciting landscape of teaching experiences that will continue well after you have graduated from your teaching program. Each phase of the portfolio-building process mentioned above has this transformation as its focus, not the physical entity that will be evaluated by your supervisors.

The Introspective Phase

The introspective phase is characterized by mulling over the act of teaching itself. You will have many questions to ponder each day as a teacher, and there's no better time to get used to such cogitations than when you are a student in the teacher education program. As a student teacher, you may not know where to start or how to think about teaching. Start by asking yourself questions in concrete everyday teaching situations, and over a period of time they will lead you to identify the teaching practices that you find appealing and effective in your mentor's practice and in your own work. Ask yourself why a teacher might teach a topic in a particular way in a particular situation. The reasons for a teacher's selection of a presentation methodology for a given topic may not be readily obvious because of the context-sensitive nature of the teaching experience and because each individual comes to teaching with his or her own leanings and field-experiences. No textbook can give you a step-by-step recipe for successful teaching. A variety of factors come into play, such as the individual student's background and preparation, language skills, and special learning needs. For example, if you were a second grade teacher who was about to introduce the concept of nutrition to your students, how would you go about it? Would you introduce it the same way to children in a fifth grade class? Would you use the same examples? Would you show them the food pyramid? Would you bring an assortment of foods to the class to taste? Would you discuss calories? After you have decided what approach you would use, list the reasons for your choice. You may realize that the audience's characteristics (school in an urban setting far away from farms) largely determined your method, but it may also have been influenced by the availability or lack of resources (parent volunteers to bring foods), or your fear that the class could deteriorate into a food-tasting party and get noisy. The introspective phase involves taking the time to ask yourself why you believe something worked, why something did not work, and what you would have done differently, and then writing down the answers.

Imagine you actually taught the class in the scenario above. You might have recorded one of the following reflections:

"This morning I taught the section on nutrition to my fifth grade students at _____ Elementary School. I had the children call out the names of their favorite foods, and we listed them randomly on the whiteboard. We then proceeded to separate the foods into food groups using the food pyramid as our guide. Class participation was excellent! At the end of the hour, parent volunteers brought in fruits, trail mix, sandwiches of various kinds, and juice. I had been a little anxious and had half-expected the students to be noisy and distracted. But they followed my ground rules for the group activity very well. I have to say the class was an unqualified success. I think it helped that I explained the ground rules and handed out roles such as group monitor, note-taker, and task-minder ahead of time. I also could not have completed this class without the help of the parent volunteers who brought in the snacks and helped pass them around."

"My fifth grade class was a little distracted today. I could not get them to pay attention to the food pyramid. I tried to get them to participate in an orderly manner by promising to hand out snacks at the end of the exercise, but made the mistake of bringing in the snacks too soon, and leaving them on the table while the lesson was in progress. It might have helped if I had enlisted a few parent volunteers to help."

Every class you take in your program and every discussion you have about teaching will offer questions to contemplate. Make it a conscious habit to spend at least 30 minutes each day, whether it's on your bus ride to school, over lunch, or curled up with your favorite beverage before bed, when you will attempt to ask and answer these questions. Later on, when you come to the end of your program and need to finish writing the statement of your teaching philosophy, the notes you make from these reflective sessions will be of immense value to you.

The "soul-searching" described above will also help you select the artifacts to meet the requirements of the portfolio. As you get more comfortable with the process of verbalizing the reasons for your choices, you will be able to write reflections on your artifacts explaining why you selected each of them. The requirements may tell you to include a sample lesson plan that was particularly effective. It will be up to you to decide which lesson plan you will include, and show how and why it was effective. It would be wise to carry with you at all times a small notebook and a pencil to jot down your realizations. As you become engaged in the portfolio process, you will find that ideas seem to occur to you "out of the blue." In fact, your brain is continually processing your experiences in the background and helping you connect the dots. The introspective phase will award your diligence and sincerity with a depth of understanding that is hard to describe. The notes that you keep from this phase will form the glue holding together the different parts of your portfolio. The introspective phase is the hardest part of building a portfolio, but also the most instructive and valuable part of the process.

The Design Phase

Katharine Cummings, Associate Dean of the College of Education at Western Michigan University, remembers with much fondness a teacher portfolio built by one of her students in the teacher education program (K. Cummings, personal communication, August 13, 2005). This was back in the early days of using portfolios as an assessment tool, when student teachers were given very few guidelines for developing their teacher portfolios. Along with the papers, case studies, and other evidence of teaching abilities, one young woman produced what she called "the teacher first-aid box." Inside the box, the student had placed a number of common items that teachers use, such as an eraser, a tape, a pair of scissors, and so on, and each item was labeled with key teaching precepts that were important to this new teacher: "A teacher must tape her prejudices outside the classroom before entering the room" and "A teacher must erase misconceptions in her students' minds." With this simple yet effective motif, the portfolio showed both the novice teacher's creativity as well as her commitment to teaching.

The process of collecting artifacts and recording your reflections will continue throughout your time in the program (and in your professional life). Meanwhile, in the design phase you start visualizing the design of your teacher portfolio. If your school uses a template, you may be limited by the order in which your artifacts need to be presented. If not, you can get creative with the ordering as well. Whether there is a formal structure or not, you will benefit from a having a theme to showcase the essence of your professional mission. This theme would be a thread that runs through your teaching practice and is exemplified by contextual examples of your work. Since a picture is worth a thousand words, using a metaphor to illustrate your work speaks volumes for what you would bring to an institution as a teacher. Whatever theme you use, make sure it is sincere and reveals who you are.

Start by listing ideas for a theme that would express your unique interests. If you play a musical instrument, you could pick a musical theme and look at the different parts of your portfolio as different aspects of a piece of music. If you like to travel, you could use that as your theme. Brainstorm for ways to build out the theme. For example, the following words come to mind when considering the metaphor of "journey": map, directions, voyage, pilgrimage, cruise, safari, adventure, trip, destination, stops, camps, milestones, stages, souvenirs, digressions, explorations, directions, meanderings, wanderings, walkabout. You can use some of these synonyms to name sections of your portfolio that will hold different artifacts illustrating the areas of your teaching proficiency. Your introduction could be a map, the conclusion could be the destination, and the other sections could be stops or meanderings along the way. Building the portfolio against the backdrop of a theme adds new dimensions to your work, and makes it fun for you as well as the reviewer.

The Implementation Phase

The implementation phase is the actual arrangement of artifacts, including the insertion of material to hold the parts together, the necessary transitions, and the presentation elements. If you have already invested the time in the first two phases, implementation becomes a smooth operation. Even though you can implement different parts of your portfolio at different times, be sure to allot enough time for the final implementation toward the end of the portfolio process as a whole. All your efforts to tell your story will be wasted if you merely string the different pieces up together in a certain order, without appropriate transitions. We'll revisit this phase in Chapter 6 when we talk about electronic portfolio software. Let's turn our attention to the contents of your portfolio.

WHAT'S IN YOUR TEACHER PORTFOLIO?

The challenge of building a teacher portfolio lies in being able to capture your teaching experiences and present them in such a way that your supervisors will have the opportunity to participate in your learning and see your transformation into a teaching professional. (You will also cherish the chance to revisit those experiences for yourself). As mentioned before, you will revisit the three phases of portfolio-building many times during this process, with the introspective phase being the hardest. The process may seem unnatural or awkward at first, and it may be helpful to think of a suitable metaphor for what you are doing. However, while you may be at a point where you have started gathering artifacts, you may not feel quite ready to come up with a metaphor for your portfolio. It is not unusual to have mixed feelings about the idea of preparing a teacher portfolio.

The process requires you to share with your reviewers ideas and perspectives that are yet to be verbalized and are still a piece of your private universe. Have you ever been a student in a class that was being observed, or been the teacher whose class was being observed? If you have, you know that this can be a nerve-wracking experience for the teacher. Many people tend to stutter or quake, or have memory lapses and panic attacks if they feel they are being watched. For the most part, this attack of nerves is based on the fear of not measuring up or of being chastised for one's inadequacies. Building a teacher portfolio and having it reviewed while you are still learning to be a teacher almost feels as if an outsider was closely scrutinizing your soul. In your portfolio, you will be asked to articulate your thoughts, approaches, and experiences to teaching situations—a tough challenge at best.

As you start building your teacher portfolio, you will have to answer some important questions, and your answers might at first feel awkward or stilted. This chapter and the one that follows will help you get past these hurdles and help you produce a portfolio that truly represents your professional development. The effort you put into this endeavor will bring rich rewards to your teaching without your even being aware of it. We'll take this exciting project forward one step at a time, making sure to record all the aspects of your teaching: context, communication, interaction with peers and mentors, feedback from your students, and most importantly, your reflections. From your reflections on your teaching practice, you will be able to formulate your teaching philosophy and begin to understand what Shulman was talking about when he called portfolio-building a theoretical act.

There are three fundamental principles of communication that are particularly relevant to your portfolio. First, a bird's eye view of your portfolio should form a part of your introduction. Provide a roadmap of the portfolio so that your reviewer knows what to expect. Each distinct section should have its own short roadmap as well. Second, anticipate your reviewer's questions and indicate where these questions will be answered. While you may not be able to glean every possible question your reviewer might raise, he or she will be impressed by the fact that you have attempted to predict his or her line of inquiry based on the purpose of a teacher portfolio. Third, provide transitions that help your reviewer move from one section to the next. Some of your reviewers may not have the opportunity to review the entire portfolio from beginning to end, since they may be involved with the portfolio process at intermediate points of development. These reviewers will appreciate the pointers you provide in your introductory account to help identify the elements of interest to them.

To help you take a collection of artifacts and transform it into a unified, whole teacher portfolio, let's start with a self-exploration exercise.

A Self-Exploration Exercise

A great way to launch the process of building your portfolio is to begin by providing some background on yourself. The questions in Figure 4.1 provide a good starting point. Use these questions to brainstorm and write down

---

Preparatory Questions

1. If you had no more than five minutes to say who you are and what you have accomplished, what would you talk about?
2. What are you passionate about?
3. Out of the many hats you have worn, which one do you identify with the most?
4. What ethical precepts guide your actions?
5. What are your plans for the future?

F I G U R E 4.1   Preparatory questions

your thoughts as quickly as they come to you, without worrying about grammar or style.

None of these questions are trivial or easy to answer. They will require you to spend some time thinking about who you are and where you are going. The answers to these questions will guide what you will include in your portfolio, the overall organization of the portfolio, and how each item will be presented. The first question helps you view your life from a bird's eye perspective. From this view, you can get closer and fill in the details as you build your portfolio. The second and third questions identify who you are. The fourth reveals the choices you would make, and the fifth helps clarify where you are going. Together, these questions spell out your mission, your vision, and your code of ethics.

You may have known from an early age that you wanted to be a teacher, and your education and experiences may reflect a clear path to your goal. Or perhaps your life has taken a more meandering path, letting you discover your passion along the way, after several changes of direction. The personal information section of your teacher portfolio will present your life as you choose to show it. If after brainstorming you are still unsure how to approach this section of your portfolio, try to construct a five-minute speech that will give your reviewers a brief history of your life. This might sound easy but it is no mean task. The challenge is to condense the key events of your life (such as where you were born, where you went to school, early leanings, favorite sports, activities, what made you choose your career, people and places that played a big role in your life) into five minutes. Since you cannot possibly relate all the details of your life in such a short time, you will find that you have to evaluate each "factoid" that you want to include against every other factoid and decide which ones stay and which ones go. This activity is a small-scale version of the reflective "review and revise" activity you will engage in as part of building your portfolio and sharpening your teaching skills in general. This will continue throughout your life as a teaching professional. The sooner you start working on your portfolio, the greater the chance to present a refined and well-orchestrated teacher portfolio. A "first-attempt" or a "written in an all-nighter" portfolio is unlikely to convince your mentors that you are ready to graduate. Further, from the perspective of your life as a professional, the value of starting the reflective process as soon as possible cannot be emphasized enough.

In a five-minute speech, you would have to be very careful when selecting details to share with the audience. You would not spend four minutes sharing a slice of your childhood, and then rush through the rest of your life in the one remaining minute. You would introduce yourself and build up to a body of detail about what is distinctive about you, and then you would finish with a concluding line that indicates where you are headed, and your hopes and dreams for the future as your professional journey continues. There would be a central theme that binds together the introduction, the body, and the conclusion—a theme you discovered when you answered the questions in Figure 4.1. Let's revisit the questions in Figure 4.1 and try to answer them. For the purposes of this exercise, let's assume you have held many positions, and have numerous talents and skills, but know now that what you really want is to be a teacher.

If you had no more than five minutes to say who you are and what you have accomplished, what would you talk about?

I would share my passion for teaching and learning, and show how being a lifelong learner has been the central motif in my life.

What are you passionate about?

I live for those moments when a concept sinks in and opens up a new world of learning to me or to the person to whom I am explaining an idea.

Out of the many hats you have worn, which one do you identify with the most?

In every job I have held, I saw myself as a catalyst who would help others succeed.

What ethical precepts guide your actions?

I believe knowledge is meant to be shared, people are the same all over the world, and it's better to be honest even if the truth is painful. Also, there's no substitute for hard work.

What are your plans for the future?

I would like to work as a middle-school teacher, teaching writing and creating classes that combine language and computing skills in a fun and exciting way. I want to make an impact on the middle-school children, as this is a critical stage in the life of a child. I am a lifelong learner and will seek out opportunities for self-development.

From these responses, it is clear that this portfolio owner is passionate about learning and wants to do more than just teach required segments from the curriculum. If you are unsure what you want to do with your teaching life, this exercise will help you understand what drives and motivates you. Think back to the various activities in which you have been involved, and find the common element that attracted you to them.

Let's assume you have answered the questions in Figure 4.1. Now think about how you would substantiate what you said about yourself. Let us suppose that it was you who said in answer to the first question "*I would share my passion for teaching and learning, and show how being a lifelong learner has been the central motif in my life.*" What does this say about your teaching philosophy? Perhaps it reveals your core belief that learning is an exchange of ideas that can happen at any age, or the fact that you are constantly looking for new and interesting things to see and do. It could also indicate that you are open to the idea of being both a learner and a teacher at the same time.

I hope you can see you how important it is to give your reviewer the big picture before getting into specific details. Now let's take our first steps in writing an introduction, a mission statement, and a statement of teaching philosophy.

Writing Your Introduction

Start your portfolio by engaging the reviewer and providing a glimpse of your foundational beliefs. Consider using a quote that you believe sums up your approach to teaching, or one that reveals your passion for teaching. Alternatively, you might include a snippet from a conversation you had about teaching with one of your supervisors or peers. Another idea is using a question that one of your students asked you and, that led to a "light bulb" moment in your teaching practice. The introduction is a good place to reveal your creativity. The ideas you include in your introduction should be personal beliefs or dispositions that apply to you and to teaching. The introduction must mark where the account of your professional journey begins, and lead on to the artifacts that will confirm and demonstrate the beliefs and methods that characterize your teaching and distinguish it from others. Your portfolio should reflect what is important to you about your choice to become a teacher and, ideally, must express your commitment.

If it is left to you to decide what information about yourself you want to include, it would be temptingly easy to just provide details in a résumé format, such as name, address, and current occupation, and a chronological rendering of the training and work experience you have had. However, your reviewers are less interested in a multitude of factoids about you than they are about the personal characteristics, qualities, and strengths that will influence how you teach. Your objective is to provide as much personal and professional information as is relevant without burdening your reviewer with information overload. Your portfolio should be a sincere account of the person you are, not a character described by the latest buzzwords. Although assessment of your skills may be the primary reason for the inclusion of teacher portfolios in your program, it helps to remember that this assessment tool is unlike other assessment tools. Here, you have the chance not just to represent your skills in the best possible way to the outside world, but also to create in this process a unique self-renewing resource for growing yourself professionally. Your portfolio becomes a rich compendium of mentored learning and, in its honesty, an exceptional marketing tool.

The artifacts you choose to include and the manner in which they are presented are very important. Ensure that your portfolio does not present an excess of detail, so overwhelming the reviewer that he or she loses touch with the main character—you. Even if a template has been provided for you, you will be able to place your unique stamp on the portfolio.

Expressing Your Mission

Your reviewers understand that your mission is to be a great teacher. The INTASC standards express a set of subsidiary goals that contribute to that end.

Your program may have an alternative way of expressing the standards. Most programs have one or more rubrics associated with their portfolio process. These rubrics are used to measure the degree to which the teacher candidate has fulfilled a particular program goal. (I address rubrics in greater detail in Chapter 6.) Study the rubrics used in your school's teacher education program. Take each goal of the program and think about how you would break it down into a set of smaller, concrete goals that are easier to accomplish. Together these goals would bring about the accomplishment of your overall mission. Develop penultimate mission statements for each section of your portfolio. These statements should a) clarify for your reviewer what you are offering in this section, and b) show that you have a clear understanding of the purpose of each part of your portfolio. As an exercise, let's take the example used earlier and formulate some mission statements for our hypothetical teacher candidate.

Broad statement of mission: *I would like to work as a middle-school teacher, teaching writing and creating classes that combine language and computing skills in a fun and exciting way.*

Some penultimate goals:

1. *I would like to develop modules to teach computer programming languages to middle-school children.*

2. *I would like to show how grammar, syntax, and logical thinking are closely interrelated.*

3. *I would like to get my students involved in research on the topic of translation and voice recognition software.*

4. *I would like to get my students involved in researching how languages develop into different regional accents.*

You can see that what starts out as a brainstorming activity slowly changes into an articulation of what excites this teacher and her motivations for teaching. Your reviewers will be much more interested in such specific details than in reading a weak statement of the obvious such as "My goal is to be an excellent teacher who can create a great learning environment."

Exploring Your Teaching Philosophy

Next, let's turn our attention to an area of your portfolio that is central to your identity as a teacher: the statement of your teaching philosophy. This entry in your portfolio is probably the most difficult artifact to produce for a number of reasons. The word "philosophy" conjures up an image of a white-haired professor seated on a chaise longue sipping a glass of wine and writing a thick volume of deep, esoteric thoughts for the betterment of humanity. I'd like to start by demystifying the word "philosophy."

It may come as a surprise to you to know that philosophy is an activity—something you "do," resulting in a set of views that may or may not at first be consistent. Philosophy is the act of applying the choices you have already made to choices you are trying to make. Further, you may not know it, but you already have the makings of a philosophy or lean towards a particular standpoint, even though you may not have considered your views about various things in relation to each other. The answers you give when prompted with hard questions about yourself, the world, and life in general are based on your philosophy. So in other words, a philosophy is a worldview you actively assume—a combination of a particular ontology or your view of being (Is the world of people and things ultimately real or just a stream of consciousness? What does it mean to say something is real?), an epistemology or a perspective on how we get knowledge (Do we get knowledge through our senses or through abstract reasoning? How can we differentiate knowledge from opinion?), and an axiology or a slant on what we consider to be a value (What are duties? What is beauty? Should the state control the individual?). Governing the activity of philosophy as a whole is logic, which helps decide whether the arguments offered in support of a view are valid or invalid, and what constitutes validity. While anyone can spout a view of the world, the view is not a philosophical system until all its concepts and theories are together internally consistent. The assumptions made by its ontology, epistemology, and axiology must fit in with each other without contradictions. Social and political thinking and theories of education usually go hand in hand with a particular ontology, epistemology, and ethics that are consistent with them. As a philosopher, you would critique other philosophers' views and expose their inconsistencies, and perhaps offer a resolution that would result in consistency.

In the course of your teacher education program, you will most likely study some of the predominant philosophies of education that have shaped current thinking on teaching and learning. As you prepare to write your statement of teaching philosophy, what you are doing is asking yourself the same hard questions that have been asked for centuries. For instance, ask yourself: What is my role as a teacher? How should I teach the segment on capital punishment? How should grades be assigned? You may have numerous unanswered questions on your mind: Is it okay to use red ink to grade assignments? Should parents help children with their homework? Can a student know more than I do in any subject? Your statement of teaching philosophy starts from exploring what is important to you in the act of teaching. How do you react to certain teaching situations? What consistent leanings do you show in your choice of teaching methods? Are there certain "givens" in your teaching style? When you have answered each question, you provide substantiating evidence to back up your answers. Here's an example of guiding principles that can be used by a teacher as the starting point for her inquiry. The comments in parentheses refer to the way these statements would be substantiated.

My teaching is guided by the following principles:

1. Respecting the student (I arrive on time, prepared for the class . . .)

2. Creating and sustaining interest (I make an effort to engage the student . . .)

3. Continuing the dialogue (my role as teacher continues outside the walls of the classroom . . .)

4. Being sensitive to student needs (I create an atmosphere conducive to individual learning styles . . .)

5. Encouraging participation (I build on students' strengths to get them involved ...)

6. Setting high standards (I set expectations properly and help my students aim high ...)

7. Making each learner feel important (I show each student that he or she matters ...)

8. Practicing what I preach (I try to teach by example ...)

From a list such as this one, you can begin to discover your teaching philosophy. It will take time to fully synthesize this inquiry, however, and for this reason, the statement of your teaching philosophy will not be the first artifact you produce in your portfolio process. However, it is a good idea to start working on this early in your program. The statement will undergo many revisions as you progress and mature in your teaching practice.

Other parts of your portfolio will relate to specific required courses you take in your program. Your professors will address those areas in depth, and you'll be able to build those areas of your portfolio on your own using some of these broad guidelines. Now that we have addressed the contents of your portfolio, you should have an understanding of what your portfolio will contain and how it will appear when completed. In the next chapter, we take an in-depth look at reflection and feedback, the essence of your teacher portfolio.

A Logistical Note

Intellectual property and privacy rights are important considerations as you build your portfolio, no matter what format (traditional or electronic) you choose. Your ideas and the ideas of those with whom you interact are intellectual property. Just as you would provide references in any other work you produce, the sources in your portfolio should be adequately documented following the reference standards supported by your institution. This includes publications, film or other media, and personal communications such as conversations or emails. As for privacy, use your discretion in sharing personal information about yourself or your family in your portfolio. Always seek permission from your sources before providing information, including photographs, on the individuals who have contributed to your portfolio.

SUMMARY

Giving your reviewer a bird's eye view of the portfolio and then providing the details is critical to the effectiveness of your portfolio. There are three important and recurring phases in the construction of your teacher portfolio: introspection, design, and implementation. Your teacher portfolio will contain numerous artifacts, some required and others that you choose to add. Each artifact should be a conscious attempt to represent your teaching abilities as well as the lessons you have learned along the way.

Here is something to consider while building your portfolio. Imagine that each day you set forth to capture some exciting vignettes from your teaching practice, and that you spent time each evening capturing your exchanges with students, supervisors, and peers in short but meaningful notes in a journal. What are the chances that a year from now you would have a rich collection of great teacher moments, snappy realizations, and in general a great, exciting year filled with things to look back on—as well as look forward to?

ENDNOTE

1. Palloff, R. M., and Pratt, K. (1999). *Building Learning Communities in Cyberspace*. San Francisco, CA: Jossey-Bass Publishers.

The Power of Reflection: Portfolio Owner as Reviewer

INTRODUCTION

In this chapter you learn how to look at your portfolio through the eyes of a portfolio reviewer. Since the heart of teaching is communication, you are continually placing yourself in the shoes of those with whom you interact (such as students, supervisors, parents, and fellow teachers). Your portfolio provides innumerable opportunities for gathering feedback from these interactions. Whether you are a pre-service or in-service teacher, it is important for you to understand the reviewer perspective. Some of the material in this chapter relates to aspects of your portfolio over which you have no control, such as the structure of the institutional template and the built-in rubrics or measures (in teacher education programs where these exist). Nevertheless, it is important for you to become intimately familiar with these "given" features of the portfolio you are building and the rationale behind them.

You may already be thinking of your portfolio as a journey that connects your current self as a teacher candidate to your future self as a professional teacher. On the way you must show mastery of a set of diverse skills, using the insights and guidance given to you by your portfolio reviewers. Although some institutions leave the construction of the teacher portfolio entirely in the hands of the candidate, many provide candidates with a portfolio template that will serve as a framework to showcase their skills. This template would have been formulated prior to the adoption of the portfolio requirement by a group of teachers and administrators. In all probability, some members of this group will also be portfolio reviewers. The discussion in this chapter is to illustrate why you need to thoroughly understand the template you are required to use (if you must use one), how to make the most of the template, and what you can do to differentiate your portfolio from those of other candidates using the same template. Even if your program does not have a formal template, you will find some useful pointers in this chapter to help you provide your reviewers with what they require from you.

As mentioned before, the portfolio process tries to mirror the intricate and reflective act of teaching. We talked about how critical it is for a teacher to examine his or her portfolio from within as well as from the vantage point of a reviewer. Throughout your career you will seek feedback from a variety of sources, including program supervisors and mentors, peers, members of the community involved with your teaching practice, and yourself. While all these forms of feedback are invaluable, your own reflections are critical to the process of mentally digesting and internalizing your teaching experience. Reflection transforms you, literally forging a growing network of neural connections that will help distinguish experienced teachers from beginners.

ADDRESSING INSTITUTIONAL PORTFOLIO GOALS

Template-Based or Free-Form Portfolios?

If your school uses a "portfolio template," you may have had an opportunity to look at the template used by your institution. Alternatively, you may be unclear about the meaning of the term. The work of designing the teacher portfolio template usually begins at least a year before the portfolio program is implemented by an institution and is entrusted to a team of educators from the teacher education program. The template is based on program goals and is fashioned by an institutional committee that will include your reviewers, and it is important for you to thoroughly understand this template.

There are several reasons why a program may choose not to use a portfolio template. The architects of the program may want candidates to be able to exercise their creativity in building portfolios, without being bound by institutional structures. Some educators believe that the portfolio should mirror the highly individual approach to teaching that each candidate is expected to bring to the profession. Your institution's assessment methodology will be tied to the template-based or free-form portfolio required as part of the teacher certification process. You will be able to learn what you need to know about the portfolio process at your institution from your supervisors and from documentation on the program's goals.

Here are some of the reasons why a program may choose to develop and use a portfolio template that will be used by all teacher candidates. First, the template ensures that none of the key elements of the teacher portfolio is overlooked. Earlier we used an architectural analogy to define the word "template," and said that the template was the structural framework supporting your portfolio. In other words, the template provides placeholders for all the parts the portfolio will one day contain. Even if you are not finishing all the rooms right away in a house you are building, you'll have planned for them by providing for plumbing, heating, electricity, and support walls. Second, requiring a common portfolio structure of all candidates adds fairness to the assessment. The candidate is freed from design tasks and is able to focus on accumulating evidence of teaching skills. You will see that it is the individuality of the artifacts and reflections you add to your portfolio that distinguish and differentiate it from others' portfolios. In our analogy, it would be easier to see which of several houses best met all the required elements of form and function if they all contained the same elements: a living room, a kitchen, two bedrooms, and a two-car garage. The way each element was rendered would make each house unique. As each part of your home is completed, it begins to acquire a character of its own that reflects your ownership.

Third, the use of a common template for use by all candidates also considerably simplifies the assessment process, because your reviewers will know where to find the portion of the portfolio they must review at a given point in the program. Just as the framework of a house would determine where the electrical outlets and network hubs will be located, the template helps designate sections within each area of the portfolio for attaching artifacts, writing reflections on the artifact, and for attaching feedback. The order of portfolio sections maps to program goals, represents an intuitive progression in the candidate's learning, or simply mirrors the portfolio committee's preferences in the order in which artifacts will be accumulated and graded.

Whatever may be the underpinnings of the construction of an institution's template, one important result of having one is that the portfolio owner is freed from the task of organizing the order of presenting artifacts. Needless to say, a lot of thought and discussion goes into the development of an institutional portfolio template. Take the time to familiarize yourself with the rationale behind the template used in your program, so that you can properly address its requirements and maximize the learning and experience you get as a candidate in the program. The template used in your program may seem more or less intuitive to you depending on your individual make-up and personality. There are many equally valid formats for a teacher portfolio template, just as there are many valid approaches to teaching. The portfolio process enables you to look at the teaching process from perspectives other than your own. It helps you comprehend the universal and yet contextual nature of the teaching experience. Understanding the template your institution uses will help you build a better portfolio.

When you take the time to understand the rationale behind the structure of the template you are required to use, you are able to visualize the completed portfolio, along with its contents. This in turn lets you plan what artifacts will be appropriate for each section long before the opportunity to collect or create the artifact presents itself. Try this "top-down" approach to portfolio development (shown in Figure 5.1) as early on in your program as possible, after portfolio requirements have been explained to you.

A TOP-DOWN APPROACH TO PORTFOLIO DEVELOPMENT

Step 1:

For template-based portfolios, make a list of the categories or sections in the template. If your school uses the INTASC-based portfolio template, you would list the ten INTASC standards in this step. If your school uses a free-form template,

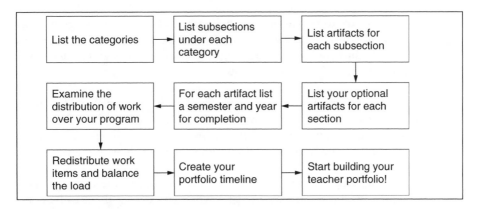

FIGURE 5.1 Top-down portfolio development

make a list of the broad areas of competence for which you will be required to offer evidence.

Step 2:

Under each section, examine the courses or subsections listed. This information should be available to you from your school's portfolio guidelines document. Alternatively, your program advisor or portfolio coordinator will be able to help you fill in this information.

Step 3:

Under each course or subsection, make a list of the required artifacts, if they exist. The required artifact will either already have been specified by the program as an assignment or activity relating to the course concerned, or you will be provided with a range or sampling of acceptable artifacts.

Step 4:

Now, using a different color, list one or two artifacts that you would like to include under each course or subsection as your optional or additional artifacts.

Step 5:

Next to each required and optional artifact, write down a date when you think this artifact will be ready in terms of a year and semester (or quarter, if your school uses the quarter system.) Note the interdependencies between artifacts, and make sure you date them accordingly. For instance, if you are required to submit a class observation of your teaching after you have taken the Teaching Methods course and have submitted a written paper (also an artifact) on a topic in that course, you know that the class observation artifact will have to wait until you have taken the course and written the paper. Be realistic about when you will be able to address this competency, in terms of your overall preparation for certification.

Step 6:

When you have listed required and optional artifacts for every area of the portfolio, assess the feasibility of your plan by ensuring that you have a good distribution of portfolio work over the period of your program. If you find that some semesters have several artifacts to be developed while some others have few or no artifacts, try to move some of the work to earlier in the program, during periods when you have less work outside of your courses. Chances are that later in your program you will be juggling much more praxis and coursework, and your plan should reflect this expectation.

Step 7:

There will be several items you can start work on right away. Schedule these early on in your plan. Such items would include general items such as your résumé, program goals, and optional artifacts from prior teaching-related work. However, expect to make changes and revisions on all of these artifacts.

Step 8:

Now draw up a timeline and list just the artifacts against the date on which you will begin work on them and the dates when you expect them to be completed. Place this timeline in a prominent location as a constant reminder, and use it to schedule your time so that you can reach your milestones as planned.

Whether or not your portfolio will be based on a template, your emphasis should be on the quality of the artifacts you include and how you bring your portfolio together. Let's revisit in depth the reflective nature of the portfolio process, as this is where quality will be determined.

THE POWER OF REFLECTION

You might recall being required by a teacher in elementary, middle, or high school to keep a journal for a reading class or perhaps a mathematics class. You may also have participated in discussion groups where you were encouraged to share your interpretation of the words of a character in a story you read. In the teaching methods course of your teacher education program, you have no doubt encountered the topic of reflection and understand why reflection is a documented part of learning. If the teacher provides opportunities for reflection, learning can happen. When we reflect on something, we pose challenges to existing patterns of thinking, and this in turn provides a way to go outside the box to a new and larger understanding.

You are learning to be a teacher, and reflection on teaching is just as important for you as reflecting on a word problem might be for your future students. Successful teachers constantly seek feedback on their teaching from their students, peers, and supervisors. As a candidate in the teacher education program and later on as a teacher, you'll receive a lot of feedback on your work from a variety of sources: teachers, supervisors, peers, students, parents, other members of the community, and yourself. The feedback will come in different formats: grades, conversations, written evaluations, formal or informal reviews, reference letters, recommendations, and your own reflections. To be an effective teacher, you must be able to take perspectives other than your own and use those perspectives to learn about your strengths and weaknesses as a teacher. You want to know how well you convey key concepts and ideas to your students and create opportunities for learning to happen. You want to be able to choose the right teaching method in each context. Some people are more inclined to be reflective than others, and reflecting on their teaching comes naturally for them. For others it is a habit that must be developed through diligent, conscious practice.

Reflection is powerful because it puts you in dialogue with yourself. You become your own critic and coach. When you reflect, what you are really doing is putting yourself in a reviewer's shoes and asking yourself some searching questions. You may not be aware of this process. Have you ever seen the main character in a play doing a monologue as he struggles to find an answer to a difficult question or an ethical dilemma of some kind? He plays devil's advocate with himself as he evaluates his options and their consequences. Reflection is a perennial source of ideas, concepts, and thoughts, limited only by the extent to which you soak up the world around you. The practice of reflection trains you to predict the questions in your students' mind. As a teacher, you are continually engaged with acts of understanding—of yourself and of other minds and of how different minds grapple with the same idea. Reflection helps you sharpen your ability to connect with someone else's understanding of an idea, and this helps you to communicate the idea in such a way that it will be understood by the individuals you are addressing.

Reflections are a big part of your portfolio for numerous reasons. They reveal your ability to connect with your students. They make you more sensitive to the needs of your students and in turn make you a better teacher. When you record reflections and return to them later on, they usually help you make other connections, and further expand your understanding. When you share your reflections with others, you enable them to see things in a way that is novel and different, and enables them to further their understanding as well. Your program may provide some guidelines for writing reflections. You will primarily be asked to submit one or more reflections on your artifacts answering such prompts as:

- What was the reason you selected this particular artifact as evidence of a particular teaching skill?
- What did you learn from the activity of creating the artifact?
- What other artifacts would you consider in the place of this artifact?

Most importantly, the reflections you add to your artifacts provide contextual evidence to your reviewer on the progress you are making in the teacher certification process.

Robertson, the professor introduced to you in Chapter 3, tells us from his experience that "shallow" reflection is a common shortcoming of teacher portfolios prepared by novice teachers. R. Robertson (personal communication, August 4, 2005). In this chapter we explore the place of reflection in portfolio development and discuss practical and effective methods to facilitate deep and meaningful reflection.

What Is Reflection?

We freely use words such as "reflection" as a part of our daily discourse, and assume that we all share in the meaning of the word. If pressed to define what

Robertson may have meant by the term "shallow reflection," each one of you might come up with a different explanation. The Merriam-Webster[1] dictionary lists the following meanings of the word "reflection":

Main Entry: **re·flec·tion**

Pronunciation: ri-'flek-shən

Function: *noun*

Etymology: Middle English, alteration of *reflexion,* from Late Latin *reflexion-, reflexio* act of bending back, from Latin *reflectere*

1: an instance of reflecting; *especially* : the return of light or sound waves from a surface

2: the production of an image by or as if by a mirror

3 a: the action of bending or folding back, **b:** a reflected part: FOLD

4: something produced by reflecting as **a:** an image given back by a reflecting surface, **b:** an effect produced by an influence (the high crime rate is a *reflection* of our violent society)

5: an often obscure or indirect criticism: REPROACH (a *reflection* on his character)

6: a thought, idea, or opinion formed or a remark made as a result of meditation

7: consideration of some subject matter, idea, or purpose

8: *obsolete*: turning back: RETURN

9 a: a transformation of a figure in which each point is replaced by a point symmetric with respect to a line or plane, **b:** a transformation that involves reflection in more than one axis of a rectangular coordinate system

– **re·flec·tion·al** *adjective*

The first four entries emphasize a new view or perspective we get on a subject by turning our thoughts upon themselves. The sixth entry ("a thought, idea, or opinion formed or a remark made as a result of meditation") expresses the value of dwelling on the same thought until new connections appear to us. The seventh entry ("consideration of some subject matter, idea, or purpose") expresses the importance of considering a subject from numerous angles. The last two entries refer to transformations. Together these entries come close to capturing the value of the act of reflection in the context of teaching. Indeed, the reflections you will be asked to include as part of your teacher portfolio will need to be much more than the statement of an idea, thought, or opinion. They will also be more than loose cogitations on a topic where you consider alternative standpoints. In fact, they will be thoughts and opinions about your work supported by reasons and examples that provide evidence of your careful consideration of the matter at hand. A shallow reflection would be unsupported statements of opinion or a restatement of the topic being considered. Such a reflection would not engender learning because it only pays lip service to the concept of reflection. Your reflections do not have to be lengthy philosophical treatises to be meaningful. They do, however, need to go directly to the heart of the issue, analyze it, and then offer a way to understand it. Your use of appropriate analogies or metaphors to explain your perspective is one indication that you are becoming the person described in INTASC standard 9 as "a reflective practitioner."

For most candidates, the practice of reflection starts as a requirement of the teacher portfolio. They have had little or no prior experience in serious reflection. The artifact itself is used as a starting point for the reflective process. It is common practice for teacher education programs to require candidates to gather artifacts for each standard adopted by the program and write a reflection on the artifact being submitted. It takes two or more attempts before a candidate is able to write a reflection that adds value to the portfolio. In between each attempt, it is helpful to have discussions with a mentor or peer about the content of the reflection, the artifact it discusses, the artifact's relevance to the standard for which it is offered, and about general guidelines for writing reflections. What connections does the reflection make? What teaching standard is exemplified here? As in the "artifactivity" exercise we examined in Chapter 3, when candidates are first introduced to the notion of an artifact, they might not immediately see that a particular artifact could be used as evidence of work supporting one or more of the several areas of required proficiency. Later, with practice, they are able to discern that what distinguishes the applicability of the artifact under one category versus another is the contextual reflection provided by the candidate on his or her choice of the artifact for the concerned category. By the second or third semester of the program, candidates have vastly amended their understanding of the word "reflection," and the term "reflective practitioner" starts to make more sense. As the saying goes, a teacher who has been teaching for ten years can have had one year of experience ten times over, or ten years of solid, reflective, teaching experience. Senior portfolio practitioners take pride in being able to participate in the transformation of a teacher candidate who goes from finding reflection hard or impossible to becoming a self-starter who can pour out meaningful reflections on her work without the need for prompts.

The Practice of Reflection

In the next few pages, we'll examine some strategies to get you comfortable with writing reflections on any topic, as well as responding verbally in impromptu conversations or discussions.

Whether you are reflecting on a theory, a method, an experience, or a work, the first step is to clear your mind of presuppositions. This means letting go of all the beliefs you hold about the subject of your reflection. For example, suppose you are asked to consider the issue of collaborative projects. There are many complex issues that must be considered, such as how a teacher should assign students to different groups so that each group will have students with different strengths when their skill sets vary considerably; what kind of ground rules could be employed to encourage participation by all the members of each group; how to ensure fairness in grading; or how to prevent cheating. The topic of group projects may be one on which you have strong opinions based on personal experience. Can you be sure that your opinions are well-grounded? If you proceed to write a reflection right away, you may paint yourself into a corner. By setting aside your opinions, you give yourself another opportunity to examine the subject with a fresh eye.

The second step is to examine the topic in a number of distinct scenarios. How would collaborative projects work with various subjects and different age groups? How do the dynamics of the group vary by level of preparation and the tasks assigned to the group? What's the context of this discussion? Think of circumstances where collaborative projects might work better and circumstances where they might not work. At this point, you are still assessing the situation. This is a good time to use strategies such as "finding the question," a method Michael J. Gelb[2] outlines in his book *How to Think Like Leonardo da Vinci*. Start by asking naïve questions that have seemingly obvious answers, and then move on to harder questions. The more questions you ask, the deeper you will go into your reflection. Write down your answers to each question, with contextual examples. Figure 5.2 lists questions you might ask:

The third step is to distance yourself from the topic so that you can see the big picture. In step 2 you finished examining it from close up. Now look at it from a "10,000 foot" view. See where the subject fits in the larger scheme of things. You'll find this sudden shift from being close to the issue to being well-removed from it to be very refreshing and productive. You'll begin to experience "Aha!" moments as you connect the dots. You'll find that your readings, the lectures you have attended, and the discussions you have had, along with your own experiences

---

1. What is a collaborative project?
2. How many people are involved?
3. Do they all do the same task?
4. Does everyone do the same amount of work?
5. What is the result of a collaborative project?
6. Does everyone get the same grade?
7. How can you tell who did most of the work?
8. Do all the groups work on the same topic?
9. What are the advantages of a group project to the student?
10. What are the advantages of a group project to the teacher?
11. Does everyone learn from a group project?
12. Does the group have the same members throughout the school year?
13. Why is a group project better then an individual project?
14. Why is an individual project better than a group project?
15. Why...?

FIGURE 5.2 Finding the question

in the field and those of your peers, come together to produce deep, meaningful reflections.

The fourth and final step is writing your reflection. If your program has provided guidelines for writing reflections, be sure to read them. If not, try leading your reviewers through the above three-step process of reflection, thus giving them a peek into your mind. Detail all the main branches of your exploration as if you were telling a story. Finish with your observations and findings, and your plans for further investigation. You'll find that reflection is a rewarding and productive activity.

Rather than waiting to be asked for a reflection on a topic, start early on in your program and pick one topic to reflect on each day. You'll be thrilled by the connections you begin to make, as your mind reacts to your stimulating inquiries. The daily practice of reflection will enable you to pick appropriate artifacts and build a great teacher portfolio. Once again, remember how your favorite professor had a way of asking just the right question or making the right statement that made you think? That is an ability you cultivate using the power of reflection. As Edison[3] said, "Genius is one percent inspiration and ninety-nine percent perspiration. Accordingly, a 'genius' is often merely a talented person who has done all of his or her homework."

Using Reflection to Select Artifacts

Remember the "artifactivity" exercise from Chapter 3? In that exercise, the challenge was to match up each of the artifacts listed with one of the ten INTASC standards. Once you become adept at that exercise, you'll find it easy to select the right artifact, out of many possible entries, for each competency. Let's discuss some strategies for matching artifacts to competencies or standards. If you already have artifacts related to teaching, you can start with the artifact and figure out which competency or standard it supports. If you are a freshman in the program, it is easier to work from the other end by examining the standard or competency and then trying to imagine examples of artifacts that would illustrate your mastery of the standard or competency.

First consider the standard or competency. Next imagine a teacher who adequately meets the requirements of the standard, and describe this teacher's style of teaching. What is it about the teacher that would reveal to any onlooker that he or she has mastered the competency in question? Give examples of what your imaginary teacher does in class or outside of it. If you needed to present this teacher's skills to someone else, what media would you use to capture these examples? Would you use class observations of his or her teaching, papers or presentations by the teacher, a video snippet of his or her teaching, sample assignments, exams, or lesson plans by the teacher? Or would you record conversations with the teacher? Your answers to these questions will point to artifacts that would be appropriate for the standard in question.

Reflection works on so many levels. A candidate may start out planning to be a teacher but later discover that teaching is not the best career choice for him or her. Another may initially want to teach middle school, but upon reflection decide that she was better suited to teaching in elementary school.

REFLECTION SELF-CRITIQUE

You can learn to review your own reflections thoroughly before you offer them to others as part of your portfolio. Let's take a closer look at some of the reflections from Chapter 3, to see if they adequately express your preparedness for a given area, or whether they can be revised. If you recall, Reflection 1 was written in support of INTASC standard 1 (Content Pedagogy), Reflection 2 in support of INTASC standard 2 (Student Development), and Reflection 3 in support of INTASC standard 4 (Multiple Instructional Strategies). The artifact they accompanied was a write-up about an activity in which the candidate participated: multi-age collaborative exercises in mathematics.

You will see that all three reflections address context to some degree and make some attempt to demonstrate the standard they claim to support. However, they all suffer from one common failing: They do not explain aspects of the activity that could have been done differently or offer alternative perspectives of the activity. Neither do they discuss where this activity stands in the overall development of the teacher candidate's preparation for certification. The questions and comments in italics are pointers for improvement from a reviewer's standpoint.

Reflection 1

"I particularly enjoyed the multi-age mathematics exercise I developed for the summer mathematics workshop. This workshop was intended to allow students from grades 2 through 5 to work together on word problems, and whet their appetite for a subject (math) that has traditionally appeared in a negative and daunting light." *Such as what? Offer examples of the exercises and specifically comment on them in relation to this reflection. Make the connection between your write-up on the activity and this reflection. Show how you understand the notion of content pedagogy.*

"The students met three times a week for a month during the summer vacation. Some of the older children found it empowering to serve as guides for the younger ones. I instructed the guides not to provide leading questions or answers but to lead their 'protégé' into discovering the solution as well as finding ways to get to the solution." *Point to examples of this that are detailed in your activity report.* "It soon became apparent to me that all children possess the ability to develop the numerical and logical skills needed for solving word problems." *What are some key educational theories about learning that may be applicable here? Have there been any new writings or research in this area?* "We worked more on breaking down the problem to manageable chunks and less on the solution itself." *Such as?* "The concept of multiplication can be understood by students in grade 2 provided they have already mastered counting and grid development exercises. This helped students overcome their fear of math." *Show some examples of this.* "I feel this artifact could apply equally to INTASC standards 1 or 2 but offer it in support of standard 1." *Were there any aspects of the activity you thought were in need of improvement? Make the connection between this experience and your overall development as a teacher.*

Reflection 2

"The multi-age collaborative mathematics exercise was one I found particularly instructive for me as a teacher." *What did you learn as a teacher?* "As the middle sibling in a family of five children, I remember accompanying my elder sisters to the candy store and watching them buy candy while Mom and Dad watched from a few feet away without becoming involved. I also learned how a pack of 18 sweets can be divided among five children (and why it was acceptable for the older children to get more!). I used the theme of a visit to the candy store in this class. I was excited to affirm that learning occurs not just in the classroom but also in social situations, in small and large diverse groups." *What are some of the other scenarios that come to mind?* "Just as, as a child, I learned how to make change for a dollar as well as experience team dynamics, the students in this class had learning experiences on more than one level—personal, social, and intellectual. I believe this artifact supports my understanding of INTASC standard 2."

Reflection 3

"I offer this artifact as an example of INTASC standard 4. I divided the class into several small groups composed of older and younger students. All the groups had access to a variety of tools and strategies for solving the word problems presented to them, such as whiteboards, pens, paper, modeling clay, beads, abacus, and grids." *Exactly what did the students do? Make the connections between your description of the activity, your expectations, and how the activity panned out.* "It was interesting to see that, regardless of age, many of these tools were used in different ways by each group." *Give concrete examples of the ways each group used the tools.* "While it is true that some of the older children showed more skill in breaking down the problem into sub-problems, it was clear that even among students with a similar level of preparation, having a variety of strategies for problem-solving was very important since each student brings his or her own unique perspective to the classroom." *Discuss some key ideas about instructional strategies, and your own development in becoming better prepared in this area. What did you learn from this activity? Would you do anything differently next time?*

SUMMARY

A template for a teacher portfolio may be developed for use by all the candidates of a teacher education program. The template can be based on skills, recognized standards, courses, or use some other format developed by the institution. Templates are helpful for portfolio owners as well as reviewers, and provide placeholders for artifacts and reflections and any other documents that need to be included in the portfolio. Reflections serve as opportunities for learning. Indeed, without reflection, no knowledge is created. Sharing reflections with the reviewer enhances your portfolio and reaps one more benefit of building your electronic portfolio. The quality of artifacts and accompanying reflections distinguish one portfolio from another, even when they are all based on the same template.

ENDNOTES

1. Retrieved September 24, 2005, from http://www.m-w.com/cgi-bin/dictionary?book=Dictionary&va=reflection&x=17&y=9.
2. Gelb, M. (1998). *How to Think Like Leonardo da Vinci*. New York, NY: Random House, Inc., p. 66.
3. Retrieved September 26, 2005, from http://www.thomasedison.com/edquote.htm.

6

Electronic Portfolio Software: So Much to Do and So Little Time!

INTRODUCTION

By this point you really understand the rationale for using teacher portfolios, a core part of a teacher certification program. You are engaged in the portfolio process and are experiencing these insights first hand. Ready to talk about an alternative format for your portfolio? How about electronic portfolio software? Why are so many educators getting excited about the idea of using electronic portfolio software to build teacher portfolios? Thinking back to our discussion from Chapter 3 where we reviewed the unavoidably digital nature of the universe we live in and its implications for the way we teach and learn, you will not be surprised that in the last few years electronic versions of teacher portfolios have become very popular. However, the new electronic portfolio is not just a digital version of a paper portfolio. Built out of software specifically intended to foster the portfolio experience, the electronic portfolio embodies the student-centered view of teaching we discussed in Chapter 2. If you have taken an on-line course, or have been required to use an on-line course-management tool in one of your regular courses for submitting assignments and receiving feedback from instructors, you will already be familiar with some of the advantages of electronic, Web-enabled tools in general. Are there additional reasons beyond Web-enablement for the growing popularity of electronic portfolio software? What can they do for you, the teacher candidate? How can you derive maximum value from the use of electronic portfolio software in building your teacher portfolio? Let's see what we can find!

ADVANTAGES OF A GOOD ELECTRONIC
PORTFOLIO SOFTWARE PROGRAM

It is common for teacher candidates to have many questions when first introduced to electronic portfolios. Is it pure hype? Oh no, do I have to learn one more software tool? The advantages of electronic portfolio software may not at first be obvious. Robertson mentions that the teacher candidates at Plymouth State University seek portfolio-related help in three areas: technical ("How do I . . . ?"), educational ("Where does this artifact fit into my portfolio?"), and functional ("Where do I put this?"). He finds that once candidates get past these initial questions, they start to think more "out of the box" while building their portfolio. (R. Robertson personal communication, August 4, 2005). Let us examine how electronic portfolio software could be advantageous to candidates and reviewers.

The Ability to Provide Artifacts in Multimedia

As a candidate in a teacher education program, you would want to offer numerous examples of the competencies you have acquired: video clips demonstrating your classroom skills, sound recordings of parent-teacher conferences, teaching tools you have developed for specific scenarios, and documents containing background information for all of these entries. After all, we are inhabitants of the Information Age, and we value information. Supporting documentation is important for credibility. With electronic portfolio software, you would be able to offer digital versions of any kind of documentation for your reviewer to examine. This is far more convenient than providing hard copies of every document.

For example, if you were a transfer student and won an award called "Student Teacher of the Year" at your former program, your reviewer would want to know more about the award—the criteria on which it was based and why you were deemed worthy of the award over your fellow competitors. It would be in your best interest to be able to provide these criteria along with your award artifact. In a world where anyone can claim expertise, these pieces of information can make a huge difference! One way to do this would be to write a description of the criteria used for the award and attach that write-up to your teacher portfolio. Another far more effective way would be to attach a document from the awarding organization with their official logo, a statement of their mission, and their explanation of award criteria. This document could be a PDF file that was made available by the awarding organization, or a photograph of the relevant page of the official award criteria and guidelines document. You could provide a hyperlink from your portfolio to the awarding organization's official Web site in case the reviewer wants to learn more about the organization. You might also want to attach a picture of the award certificate. Any of these options would be easy to orchestrate with the electronic portfolio software.

We appreciate rich contextual information, but we also live very busy lives. Consider another common scenario. Suppose you wanted to have your reviewers observe your classroom management skills, but were unable to find a mutually convenient time and place to do so with each reviewer. You could have someone videotape your class or classes and attach the video clips to your electronic portfolio. If you were still using the paper portfolio, you would have to circulate the videotape or make copies of it to circulate to your reviewers. The media-rich nature of electronic portfolio software renders the logistics of getting evidence to your reviewers a smooth and seamless activity.

The Ability to Dispense with Any Form of Hard Copy

If the electronic portfolio software is Web-enabled, you would provide your reviewers with a Web site hyperlink to your portfolio. This would altogether remove the need to provide a copy of your portfolio to a reviewer in any form—whether paper or a digital format such as a CD-ROM or DVD. You will continually add artifacts to your portfolio over the course of the teacher education program. Not all of your reviewers will review your portfolio every semester, but a few will. You will want to be able to share the entire portfolio in its metamorphosis. A Web-enabled format will let you do this without having to make additional copies of your portfolio every time it is updated. The artifacts you attach to your electronic portfolio will be saved in a database and "served up" when you or your reviewer click on a link to view them. You can dispense with the need to carry around a heavy and voluminous tome!

The Ability to Plan Your Portfolio-Building Time in Small Buckets

You have so much to do and so little time. With the paper portfolio, you would have to be at a specific location where the portfolio is located (home or work) to work on your portfolio, or get used to carrying around your heavy tome. With electronic portfolio software, you can work on your portfolio at any time and place that you use your computer, and thereby use your time—that scarcest of resources—much more fruitfully. You'll find that spending 15 minutes a day in portfolio-building can easily be worked into your busy day—over a cup of coffee, between classes, while waiting for your ride, in a waiting room, or wherever you have a few minutes on your hands. With a Web-enabled portfolio program, the reviewer benefits from the same advantage and can work on your portfolio from any place with Internet access, whether it is work or home, without needing to carry your manuscript around. The electronic portfolio fits in well with today's need for "multitasking."

The Ability to Present Your Information
in Easy-to-Absorb Formats

Another time-saving, reviewer-friendly feature of electronic portfolios is their nonlinear presentation of materials and the ability (with a well-developed template design) to layer information and avoid information overload. In the case of a teacher portfolio, the amount of information required to make a fair assessment of a candidate's teaching abilities can get voluminous. This could make the paper portfolio quite overwhelming to the reviewer. The primary drawback of a linear format is that it is flat and one-dimensional. Events are ordered by date in different categories. Length is a serious consideration. It is difficult for the reviewer to separate or order the entries using criteria other than their place in the timeline. Hence major milestones are situated side by side with less significant achievements. It is difficult to explain gaps in time when the individual was engaged in pursuits other than professional or academic ones, however challenging or worthwhile they might have been. Hyperlinked nonlinear formats are more user-friendly, as anyone used to surfing the Internet will tell you. An electronic portfolio allows the reviewer to follow his own line of inquiry rather than be restricted by the presentation, and relieves the tedium of information overload.

A good electronic portfolio software package will let you organize your materials in customized, intuitive layers. Layers add depth and offer some key advantages. First, your reviewer gets to know you one important piece at a time, without being bombarded with a data blitz. Second, the reviewer is able to choose the elements in which he or she is most interested, as each layer provides structure and visibility to the layers that lie below. At first you may find it difficult to imagine any way of organizing your materials other than the usual linear arrangement of topics. Let's re-visit the self-exploration exercise in Chapter 4 when you were asked to construct a five-minute speech about yourself. Taking the outline of the speech you prepared, select the categories and the subcategories you want to share with the reviewer. Now stack the subcategories under the main headings in such a way that the reviewer will be able to see the big picture and drill down as desired.

For practice, let's assume you want to include all of the information listed in the following figure:

Figure 6.1 shows a layered rendering of some of the same information. Let's create a category called Personal Data. Next, let's create as many sublayers as we need to present this information to the reviewer. Some of the sections have been expanded as an example.

Figure 6.2 shows how you can add depth to your portfolio, and at the same time give the reviewer the opportunity to pick the artifact in which he or she is most interested. If the portfolio software is truly user-friendly, you also provide visibility to the entire contents of the section on Personal Information without having to use your mouse to drill down into each layer before it becomes visible. Providing visibility saves the reviewer from a tedious waste of time and information overload.

The opportunity for adding richness and depth offered by an electronic portfolio software program helps avoid the "checklist" orientation—a factor that could be detrimental to a portfolio program. Instead of being a compilation of artifacts, your teacher portfolio can now become a living documentary of your experiences.

The Ability to Keep Your Portfolio Current

If you are using an institutional template, you can utilize the built-in rubrics and feedback areas to the fullest extent. Electronic portfolio software helps create a

Examples of Personal Data:
Names by which you have been known
Address
Email and phone number
Personal philosophy
Cultural background
Family history
Reflections on personal characteristics
What others have said about you
Hobbies
Activities
Sports
Social activities and clubs
Community service

Examples of Academic Data:
Subjects studied
Schools attended
Degrees or certifications
Accrediting bodies
Program outcomes
Plans for further learning
Projects and assignments completed in school
Participation in student government
Membership in student organizations
Sports activities
Publications

Examples of Work-Related Data:
Positions held
Roles held in different positions
Responsibilities held
Companies or organizations who employed you
Projects completed
Career objectives or goals
Work-related mission statement
Code of ethics
Hard skills
Soft skills

FIGURE 6.1 Personal information

"live" portfolio. In a paper–based portfolio, although you can add reflections on an activity, there are logistical limitations on capturing continuing dialogues on the topic. When you use electronic portfolio software, you can continually capture ongoing dialogues and reflections on your progress in the program. Feedback is captured along with the name and role of the person providing the feedback and time stamped to provide a point of reference. When additional comments are added, their timestamp clarifies the context of the latest insights, rather than appearing as random additions. By participating in a dialogue with your reviewers on the reflections area of your portfolio, you can illustrate the strides you are making in your understanding.

Personal Information (Description: My personal values, the many hats I wear in my personal life, and where you can reach me)

   Personal Philosophy (Attachment: A short document on my personal philosophy)

   Favorite Quotes (Attachments: Pertinent Web links)

   Role Models

      Bill Cosby (Attachment: Short document about this role model)

      Mahatma Gandhi (Attachment: Short document about this role model)

      Helen Keller (Attachment: Short document about this role model)

   Mentors (Attachments: Short document about my mentors)

Personae

   Professional

   (to be expanded into layers)

   Family (Description: The different roles I play in my family)

      Mother, daughter, sister (Attachment: Documents explaining each role)

   Artistic

      Writer (Attachments: Information about stories/books I have written, attachments: awards won)

      Musician (Attachments: Web links to information about the band I play in, attachments: audio clips of my music)

      Dancer

         Ballet (Attachment: Information about my accomplishments in this area)

         Tap (Attachment: Information about my accomplishments in this area)

Activities

   Community service

      Coordinator, Summer Reading Program (Attachments: Documents, Web links about the program)

   Hobbies

      (Attachments: Special achievements or collections)

   Sports

      (Attachments: Awards won, games played, level)

Contact Information

   Address

   Phone numbers and email

Citizenship (description of your status)

Names

   Official

   Nicknames

   Other aliases

References

   (Attachments: Contact info for references)

   (Attachments: Web links to professors' home pages)

   (Attachments: Letters of reference)

FIGURE 6.2 Personal information layered

The Ability to Help Your Institution Maintain High Standards

Your school will explain the rationale of the institutional template they have devised for the teacher education program. It is important that you understand the structure of the template you will be required to use. Once you familiarize yourself with the measures, rubrics (a scoring guide or rating schema), and standards used by your institution, you will be able to build your portfolio so that it will represent your best attempt to capture your teaching abilities.

Perhaps the most important advantage offered by an electronic portfolio software program is the ability to have built-in rubrics enabling you—the candidate—to understand and participate in the assessment process. When the program's larger objectives are phrased in specific contextual guidelines and these guidelines are readily available as part of the portfolio, you are afforded the best opportunity for success. You will be able to revisit the criteria side by side with the submitted artifact and the reviewer's assessment. This will help you understand your reviewer's comments and learn from the experiences depicted in the artifact. A portfolio rubric used by Plymouth State University[1] uses a four-point scale to assess three areas of the teacher portfolio: résumé, technology, and artifacts (see Table 6.1). Reflections on artifacts are also assessed for writing and content.

Embedded rubrics make the task of reviewing a portfolio easier and keep feedback meaningful and within immediate reach. When a template has embedded rubrics, the portfolio owner has specific guidelines with which to work, and the result is vastly improved skill sets and a portfolio that reflects the program's goals in a concrete way. Thus a good electronic portfolio program can indirectly impact the quality of the educational experience at your institution and help keep standards high.

EARLY DIGITAL PORTFOLIO FORMATS

Early electronic portfolios were typically Web sites where teacher candidates shared their teacher portfolios with their reviewers, or teacher portfolio documents were saved as files on a CD-ROM or DVD and submitted to reviewers. Although these digital formats were in many ways an improvement over the hard-bound paper portfolio, they still suffered from some serious drawbacks.

First, they placed the less technologically savvy candidates at a disadvantage, as they required familiarity with building Web sites from scratch either with a programming language or through the use of graphical user interface (GUI) tools such as Microsoft FrontPage™. Teacher candidates now had to add advanced technical proficiency to the long list of skills they needed to master. Since presentation played a big role in portfolio evaluation, the less sophisticated Web sites tended to rate poorly compared to the more flashy ones, taking the focus away from the main purpose of a teacher portfolio, namely the candidate's

TABLE 6.1 Plymouth State University Electronic Teacher Portfolio Rubric

	Exceeding 4	Accomplished 3	Developing 2	Beginning 1
Resume	Complete, very descriptive, yet succinct, includes a variety of action verbs, consistent format, visually pleasing.	Complete, somewhat descriptive, includes some action verbs, consistent format, easy to read.	Incomplete, vague descriptions, passive constructions, inconsistent format, visually cluttered.	Incomplete or missing components, inadequate descriptions, passive constructions, inconsistent format, visually cluttered.
Artifacts	Excellent variety of artifacts that clearly illustrate the candidate's growth personally and/or professionally.	Artifacts show some variety, but not as wide of range as level 4.	Artifacts have little variety and do not fully represent the candidate's growth personally and/or professionally.	Artifacts have no variety and do not represent the candidate's growth personally and/or professionally.
Artifact Reflection: Content	Reflective pieces clearly put artifacts into context, make strong connections to CHECK*, provide in-depth analysis of personal and/or professional growth.	Reflective pieces put artifacts into context, make some connections to CHECK, provide some analysis of personal and professional growth.	Reflective pieces put artifacts somewhat into context, make limited connections to CHECK, provide limited analysis of personal and professional growth.	Reflective pieces do not put artifacts into context, make little or no connections to CHECK, provide limited analysis of personal and professional growth.
Artifact Reflections: Writing	Reflections demonstrate superior control of the conventions, usage, and sentence structure of written English, use rich vocabulary to convey meaning.	Reflections show adequate sentence variety and occasional use of rich vocabulary, some mechanical errors that do not interfere with meaning and have appropriate language usage and sentence structure.	Reflections show limited sentence variety and repetitious vocabulary, mechanical errors, and sentence structure interferes with meaning.	Reflections show rudimentary sentence variety and vocabulary, mechanical errors eclipse meaning, and sentence structure interferes with meaning.
Technology	Uses a variety of technological innovations (scanning, digital camera); sophisticated use of technology and clearly appropriate for task. All required artifacts are included and placed in their proper location in the electronic portfolio, completely revised.	Uses technology, but not as varied as level 4 (scanning); appropriate for task required, artifacts are included and placed in their proper location in the electronic portfolio.	Attempts limited technological innovation (word processing); inappropriate for task. Two required artifacts included and placed in the proper location in the electronic portfolio.	No attempt at technological innovation to effectively use technology. One or no required artifacts included and placed in the proper location in the electronic portfolio.

* CHECK is Plymouth State University's Conceptual Framework for Teacher Education. The acronym stands for Commitment, Holism, Experience, Collaboration, Knowledge.

teaching skills. Some programs merely required candidates to use a word-processing program such as Microsoft Word™. Although the technical complexity was greatly reduced, the functionality was reduced as well.

Second, regardless of one's technical abilities, maintaining portfolios on Web sites demanded a lot of time and effort for managing both technical and content changes. The need to build a sophisticated Web interface to represent the candidate's teaching artifacts took time away from the more important aspects of the portfolio process. For portfolios on CD/DVDs, there was the additional problem of having to duplicate media for multiple reviewers to review the portfolio. Further, since teacher portfolios would need to be reviewed at regular intervals in the course of the program, the candidate's work would be submitted in pieces, and giving continuous feedback on the candidate's work was well-nigh impossible.

The third and most severe shortcoming of both these electronic formats was that the assessment process was completely separate and outside of the portfolio. Even if all of the pieces of the portfolio were presented together, the reviewer had no way to submit assessments and feedback on the Web site. He or she would have to submit these assessments in separate documents. Even though the digital format allowed for the inclusion of multimedia files and offered the reviewer a nonlinear view of the teacher portfolio, the users (candidates and reviewers) were not able to seamlessly communicate via interconnected networks that would enable more direct interaction. Electronic portfolio software promised not only to overcome these limitations, but also deliver to the portfolio process a windfall of conceptual advantages.

However, this promise was not immediately realized. The first electronic portfolio programs were glitchy and formulaic. As with all software, it would not be until the electronic software market matured that truly functional, full-featured, electronic portfolio software programs would come into being. Today we have several competing electronic portfolio software products that an institution might consider for use in a teacher education program. To make an educated choice among these products, one needs to consider the features that one could reasonably expect in a solid, pedagogically supportive electronic software program. A good electronic software program that will be used in teacher education programs should provide for the following as part of its standard offerings:

- Robust, Web-enabled, user-friendly architecture
- Portfolio process–oriented functionality:
  - Templates
  - Standards, rubrics, and benchmarks
  - Easy management of media-rich artifacts
  - Ease of review
  - Security and data integrity
  - Ease of gathering student performance data by the institution

In the next section, we illustrate the use of these features in evaluating an electronic portfolio software program. Why should you be interested in this section? There are several reasons.

Several schools have student representation in the committee that selects software. You yourself may have the opportunity to be involved in the electronic portfolio software selection process at your institution. If so, the next section will enable you to contribute to the selection process. However, even if you are not currently involved in the software selection process, you will be able to use the valuable insights on electronic portfolio software provided in this section to maximize the value of the tool as you build your first electronic portfolio. Looking further ahead in your career, you may have your own students building learning portfolios. These may be traditional or electronic. Based on the growing trend to use digital portfolio formats and particularly electronic portfolio software, arming yourself with a thorough conceptual understanding of this genre of software would be well advised. (Appendix 1 gives you a sampling of the features of an electronic portfolio software program in use today.)

EVALUATING ELECTRONIC PORTFOLIO SOFTWARE

Robust and User-Friendly Architecture

To start with, the software must be easy to use, with a user-friendly, intuitive, graphical user interface. It must be functional, whether you are a technical wizard or a first-time computer user. It must not demand extensive training. It must use standard icons and symbols that you are accustomed to seeing on other widely available programs. It must be straightforward to install and be accessible at all times, day or night. It must be robust and reliable, so that users can upload their artifacts with ease and expect to find them there each time they return to work on their portfolio. It must be easy to update, remove, or add artifacts, and operate seamlessly without crashes or loss of connectivity. Keeping in mind that no software is perfect, it must operate without serious glitches or the constant need for "workarounds." It must be secure so that you can feel comfortable in your own private workspace. You must be able to download your accumulated work to an alternate storage medium such as a CD-ROM or DVD or a computer hard disk if you choose to do so, during or after completion of your teacher education program. In short, using an electronic portfolio software program should not require any more proficiency in using technology than is already in demand for a teacher today.

The software must enable you as a candidate to take ownership of your portfolio, and enable you to enjoy the work of building your teacher portfolio. When you update your portfolio, you must be able to see the changes right away. Logging into and out of the portfolio must be quick and easy, so that you can work on your portfolio at a time that is convenient to you. You should not need to pull all-nighters building your portfolio because the software server was "down" or unavailable when you had tried to access it. The software must work across different hardware and operating system platforms, so that the kind of computer you own does not matter. You must not be required to purchase additional support software to run this program. The software must also be affordable for candidates.

Portfolio Process–Oriented Functionality

Templates The software must make it easy to design, build, and modify numerous institutional templates for teacher portfolios. As the portfolio owner, you should be able to create one or more portfolios as their need dictates, based on a template or otherwise. You should have the option of using an institutional template that is available to you (if required by the program) or easily create your own design structure with sections to hold the artifacts you will attach. By supplying a predefined framework, look, and feel, the use of a template levels the playing field for all candidates, freeing them to focus their attention on teaching skills.

In previous chapters, we talked about how many schools use INTASC standards as the basis of their teacher portfolio template. We also mentioned that an institution can fashion its template out of core competencies, courses, or any set of premises that they deem fundamentally relevant to the teacher certification process. Template-building is a collaborative activity in which a group of educators consider ways to capture the steps that lead to the accomplishment of the primary goal of their teacher education program: producing good teachers. Template-building should have been completed and finalized before teacher candidates are introduced to the electronic portfolio program. The rationale underlying the concept of a template must be explained to candidates from the start.

Standards, Rubrics, and Benchmarks The templates designed using the electronic software program must support key requirements from the perspective of the teacher education program. They must support the purpose of the teacher portfolio by facilitating effective assessment structures. They should provide for the addition of standards, rubrics, and benchmark information, and have a designated area for candidate reflections and reviewer feedback.

Embedded rubrics governing the way candidate work will be assessed give electronic portfolio software a unique edge over other portfolio formats. We looked at an example of such a rubric earlier in this chapter. Where necessary, the template should be able to provide samples, standards information, or benchmarks so that you will have a way to measure your own work before it is submitted to be reviewed by one of the program reviewers. The software used must be flexible enough to serve the needs of the program and allow the inclusion of these elements. The teacher education program must not have to shape itself to the limitations of the software.

Easy Management of Media-Rich Attachments As portfolio owner, you should be able to attach a wide variety of media, including Web links, video, and sound files, so that text, pictures, photographs, graphs, spreadsheets, and other data can be attached as evidence of work completed in the program. The process of attaching artifacts should be streamlined to allow you to browse to your hard disk and upload the documents into a secure personal archive or collection created for your exclusive use on the portfolio server. There must be a way to manage these attached artifacts. If an artifact is attached to multiple parts of a portfolio or more than one portfolio, you should be warned when you attempt to delete the attachment. There should be a way to remove an attachment without deleting it from the archive. If you want to attach an artifact to a different section of the portfolio or to a completely different portfolio, you should not have to start all over again from the upload process. It must be easy to alter or add explanatory notes and narratives to any part of the portfolio.

You must have a chance to submit an improved version of the artifact reviewed, if this is a part of the institution's portfolio ground rules. The ability to redo and resubmit a piece of work and attach the resubmission as an artifact that illustrates the progress made by the candidate is a particularly powerful feature that electronic portfolio software offers over other formats of portfolio development and submission.

Ease of Review   There should be an easy way to add or remove reviewers through the course of the program, since the portfolio may be reviewed by different reviewers as it develops. There must be a reliable way to share the portfolio with one or more reviewers when the portfolio is ready to be shared. You must be able to control which of your reviewers can provide feedback on the portfolio in the designated areas, and which of the reviewers may only access the portfolio in "read-only" mode. You must also control whether the feedback from one reviewer can be seen by other reviewers while they are reviewing the portfolio. It is critical for the electronic portfolio process to facilitate the impartiality and independence of a reviewer's feedback by isolating it from the feedback of other reviewers while the candidate is making their way through the program. There must be a way for the portfolio to be reviewed in parts or in its entirety—artifacts, reflections, reviewer feedback, and all—by a "super-reviewer" such as a program director or advisor at the end of the program. The built-in rubrics mentioned earlier can provide a way to avoid potentially conflicting reviewer feedback on any given artifact. Since a reviewer could approach the portfolio from a particular perspective, at a given point in the program, and the same artifact could be used to demonstrate multiple areas of proficiency, well-defined rubrics are essential to the portfolio process.

Security and Data Integrity   The integrity of the portfolio must be preserved. There must be safeguards in place to prevent changes to completed portions of the portfolio while it is being reviewed and after the assessment has been completed. For example, having the portfolio owner lock down his or her portfolio prior to review, and having the portfolio reviewer unlock the portfolio after the review might be one way to ensure that the portfolio owner/reviewer interaction is a mutually satisfactory process, meeting the rigor of academic assessments. Reviewers must not be able to directly edit or modify the artifacts themselves. Their role must be restricted to providing feedback on the version of the artifact submitted.

Ease of Gathering Student Performance Data by the Institution   While most of the features discussed above pertain directly to you as a portfolio owner and to your reviewers, there's an institutional advantage in using electronic portfolio software that indirectly benefits you. If the institutional template is well-planned with such features as embedded rubrics, it is possible to get a measure of teacher candidate performance from the aggregate of student portfolios. This data collection could be conducted in a secure manner without violating the privacy of individual portfolios, just as data on student performances can be obtained from the aggregate data from standardized tests. The results could be used by the institution (to strengthen its programs and ensure that program goals are being met), and by accrediting bodies and state licensing organizations (to ensure that institutions maintain the highest standards). The fact that data-gathering of this kind is made possible could potentially set in motion an all-around institutional effort for higher standards, such as increased participation in the portfolio process by faculty, administrators, and the community, and greater responsiveness to candidate needs.

In a nutshell, the software must support the assumptions of the portfolio process we outlined in Chapter 1: be a repository of program-long work by teacher candidates that at any time reflects their level of progress in the mastery of teaching skills; provide contextual examples of teaching abilities through the inclusion of a variety of media; allow for an expression of ongoing collaborative interchanges such as peer feedback and responses; be an effective way to capture lessons learned through mentoring and coaching mechanisms; and support the development of a teaching identity expressing understanding based on deep reflection. Ideally, your teacher portfolio should lend itself to extended maintenance and development as you continue on in your professional life.

FUTURE DIRECTIONS FOR ELECTRONIC PORTFOLIOS

From working closely with both educators and teacher candidates, and assuming a key role in the introduction of an electronic portfolio program at his institution, Robertson has heard both sides of the argument for and against electronic portfolios. He has this to say of where he thinks electronic portfolios are headed:

> The next generation for electronic portfolio systems is to integrate Web services that help portfolio owners express themselves. The more creativity and personality that can be interjected, the more potential ownership the student will take in the portfolio itself. Electronic portfolio systems have the potential to strike deeper at the heart of student learning because the student is the center of work. Course management systems are very faculty-centered. Faculty members build the experience for students to participate in. In the ideal electronic portfolio, the student builds the experience for faculty, advisors, friends, employers, etc., to participate in. (R. Robertson personal communication, August 4, 2005.)

The world is so intricately networked now that we are not even aware of it. Information technology seamlessly connects user to user, school to school, and organization to organization. But it goes even further. We can talk across departments, across platforms, across domains, and across disciplines. Along the way we have abandoned technologies that isolate segments of our lives and replaced them with technologies that integrate. Electronic portfolio software that looks ahead to this need to integrate different dimensions of our lives gives us a better understanding of ourselves and each other. Technology that does not recognize our need to view life as a continuum would soon fall into obsolescence.

We want to use, reuse, and recycle. We certainly do not want to reinvent. We want to save valuable natural resources by reducing or eliminating paper and energy waste. We want to collect data once and share it in a secure way across different domains, as needed. We want to make our lives more streamlined and more efficient so that we can make time to enjoy our leisure activities.

There are still numerous questions that remain. How will the portfolio review process change assessment in general? Does a portfolio ever reach a state of "completion" or will it always be a "work in progress"? Perhaps you will help answer some of these questions after you graduate from this program and become a full-fledged teaching professional in your own right. As the benefits of electronic portfolios begin to be felt, we may witness paradigm changes in educational practices in areas such as assessment. Will these changes bring us closer to the realization of a learning society? We take a look at these cultural changes in the next and final chapter.

SUMMARY

Electronic portfolio software can offer tremendous advantages to the portfolio process in terms of richness of media, ease of access, templates, built-in rubrics, and logistics. It can transform the teacher education process into a student-centered experience that is in sync with the digital, networked universe in which we find ourselves today.

ENDNOTE

1. Rubric used in Plymouth State University Education Department Childhood Studies Electronic Portfolio template (2005).

7

In Conclusion

INTRODUCTION

We have covered a lot of ground and our journey together is almost over. If you have been following the suggestions in this book, you may already have started working on your teacher portfolio. In this concluding chapter, we have two primary objectives. First, we look at the cultural implications, if any, of the widespread adoption of electronic portfolios. We try to answer some of the questions you may have: What can we derive from our experiences with teacher portfolios that would be equally meaningful in domains other than teacher education? How are electronic portfolios being used outside teacher education, and how does their application in other realms in turn impact our future interaction as teaching professionals with electronic portfolios?

Second, we examine sample artifacts form the portfolios of teacher candidates and professional teachers, and get a better understanding of the value of using electronic portfolio software. After we have armed you with these ideas, our work is done, and we leave you to continue your exciting journey of discovery in teaching—a journey that we hope will continue through the rest of your life.

PORTFOLIO USE IN TENURE AND PROMOTION

In Chapter 2 we talked about the need for teacher accountability and professionalism as one of the major triggers of the portfolio movement. In Chapter 6 we looked at the institutional ramifications of using portfolios. It would appear that the earnest adoption of teacher portfolios as an assessment tool by an institution engenders accountability at all levels. We are able to gather and present concrete contextual evidence of teacher development and growth, and the acquisition of necessary skills for certification or promotion. Portfolio-based evidence adds to and corroborates other more traditional forms of assessment such as written and multiple choice–based board examinations, and face-to-face interviews. However, portfolio programs offer opportunities to transcend these assurances at the level of individual teacher preparation. For pre-service teachers, they shed light on the institution's accountability to the candidates in its program, by requiring a formalization and a mutually convenient documentation of the coaching and mentoring process during the pre-service period. For in-service teachers, when portfolios form part of the promotion and tenure process, these gains are multiplied. Xu's paper provides an excellent case study of the benefits of using teacher portfolios for professional development for teachers in an urban elementary school.[1] Some of the beneficial results of professional learning and collaboration mentioned are: teachers taking more time to examine their own approaches to teaching; teachers taking more risks to find new and effective teaching strategies; teachers becoming more responsive to their students; teachers finding new opportunities to connect with their peers; administrators getting to understand their teachers better; improved communication and an overall sense of increased participation in the academic community.

"When carefully conceived, portfolios can significantly advance a teacher's professional growth. They can also ensure that evidence of exemplary teaching doesn't vanish without a trace."[2]

THE ELECTRONIC PORTFOLIO MOVEMENT

We started out in an attempt to understand why portfolios are an awesome assessment tool for teacher education. Although portfolios have been distinguished into different kinds based on whether they are for showcasing one's skills, for employment or assessment, or as an example of one's evolving skill set, our study of the teacher portfolio showed that all of these purposes can be met depending on how the portfolio program is implemented. We saw how they can be used to chart your progress, showcase your accomplishments, and—most importantly—enable professional growth in ways no other tool can do. We saw that the recognition of the value of portfolios for academe has led to their use in teacher hiring, faculty tenure, and promotion, and in documenting how well an institution is meeting its stated program outcomes. Extending this idea, we saw that portfolios support institutions in maintaining high standards, securing grants from national bodies or private organizations, and maintaining institutional accreditation. As you might have guessed, these benefits are just as applicable outside of teacher education, even where portfolios are not yet used as an assessment methodology.

Portfolios hold tremendous potential across the board. In an earlier chapter, we mentioned the use of portfolios in the world of art, business, and other vocational fields for showcasing one's accomplishments and for filling job openings. People in all professions—whether medicine, sports, law, or architecture—could use portfolios to tell their individual or organizational story, the way individuals in artistic or creative professions involving multimedia already do. Portfolios could be a great way to catalogue one's lifetime achievements, at whatever level one desires—individual, team, family, community, organization, or some other dimension. Coming full circle, this trend toward the widespread use of portfolios in areas other than teaching gives you a head start in portfolio development. Not only will you continue to use portfolios in your professional life, you will also be able to assist members of the community who are venturing into portfolios for the first time.

The Hiring Process

Electronic portfolios are an ideal way for Human Resources (HR) in any organization—academic or corporate—to find the right candidate. In a world of electronic document submittal and automated prescreening before interviews, both employers and jobseekers today have to deal with "buzzwords" and "word-smithing." You could be an awesome candidate, but get eliminated by the software used to scan your résumé for keywords, because of your choice of words. Conversely, someone with far less education and experience than you could make it to the second level (face-to-face or phone interview) because their résumé is cleverly crafted to include all the necessary buzzwords. The HR department has a key role to play in working with the academic hiring committee to ensure that the right candidate is selected in a fair and open way. So it works in your favor that portfolios are beginning to be perceived as valuable tools by your academic peers and supervisors, as well as nonacademic HR personnel involved in the hiring process. The HR department will continue to be involved with your professional life by participating in the method used to track your career after hiring, with the tenure and promotion committee. They may help recognize your widening skill set in numerous areas, including soft skills development (such as communication skills, team-building skills, and conflict resolution) and subject matter expertise, and be involved in ensuring that your value as a human resource is upheld.

Portfolios provide a good platform for such assessment because they can provide contextual examples to illustrate the employee's skills and expertise, rather than relying on hearsay or standardized testing. (Standardized testing may not even be feasible in some careers.) Individuals can use electronic portfolios for career development, job searches, and personal goals tracking. At a team level, portfolios hold the potential for being used as learning tools for projects, especially in long-term projects involving major milestones. There is a trend in industry toward what is called "matrix" reporting, where instead of working for a single supervisor, an employee becomes a resource that is available to multiple departments within the company. The increase in interdisciplinary activities in academe indicates that educational institutions would greatly benefit from the matrix approach. Instead of teachers or professors belonging to a given department, they could be an institutional resource and work for any department that can use their skills. The HR department can track, identify, and reward faculty who have done coursework or praxis to widen their proficiencies. The ability to know what resources are available within the institution could be made easier when the school has a portfolio-based assessment and evaluation platform. From the perspective of the individual teacher, portfolios provide the ideal platform for continued reflective self-development and professional growth. Based on these advantages, it seems likely that more and more institutions will use portfolios for tenure and promotion.

A major impetus in institutions today is the expressed mission to recognize the worth of each individual's contribution to the growth of the institution. This goes with the need for instilling an understanding of desired outcomes for the school's goals at the level of the individual employee. Most organizations—whether for-profit or nonprofit—have a central mission and vision. To achieve that mission, every member of the team must participate in actions conducive to the mission. The supervisors of each department are entrusted with ensuring this participation at the individual level. Portfolios can demonstrate work done toward a common goal in a telling way. For example, in a large public school system, a high school can build a portfolio showcasing the achievements of its teachers in supporting a community goal. One of the artifacts might be the efforts to raise funds for building a community recreation center. Another might be the students' participation and performance in the national spelling bee. Portfolios representing each school in the district can be used as a powerful way to showcase alignment with the school system's mission, as well as recognition of individual contributions to the team.

Additionally at the organizational level, an organizational portfolio can be used for marketing purposes to compete for government or private contracts. The potential for community building through a shared community portfolio that tracks community events and milestones is not difficult to imagine. As with individuals, institutions, and corporations, towns and communities need mechanisms that will help them assess how successful or unsuccessful their initiatives have been. There's increased participation today between institutions and communities, governments and businesses. Again, these partnerships can benefit from the use of a portfolio program. The fact that interdisciplinary initiatives could cross academic and corporate boundaries further underscores the value of using portfolios.

However, one factor above all else reinforces the spread of portfolio use in all realms: the growth and availability of information technologies. The explosion in Web-enabled tools rendered easily accessible through computer networks and media that spawn the entire globe have turned "wish-list" items into items of common everyday use. (Less than ten years ago, dial-up was the only option for connecting to the Internet. The idea of being able to download music and be on the phone at the same time over the same data communications channel would have been deemed wishful thinking.) The ideas expressed on the Science Fiction channel do not seem as far-fetched anymore with the advent of such things as GPS systems as standard features on cars and the ability to get the latest news anywhere anytime. Technology has added new dimensions to established and valued practices such as storytelling, art, drama, and cultural expression of other kinds by rendering them in the "virtual" realm of cyberspace. For example, digital storytelling is a new field that offers opportunities for varying levels of user participation in the story, using electronic media. Instead of being a passive observer, you could potentially participate using advanced software to change the outcome of the story. The fear that computers would dehumanize our lives is countered by the realization that technology can bring the world closer in new and exciting ways, enable us to learn more about each other than ever before, and increase the value of the human resource. Put it all together and you have powerful tools—such as electronic portfolio software—now available to fill a growing range of needs. With the desire for greater

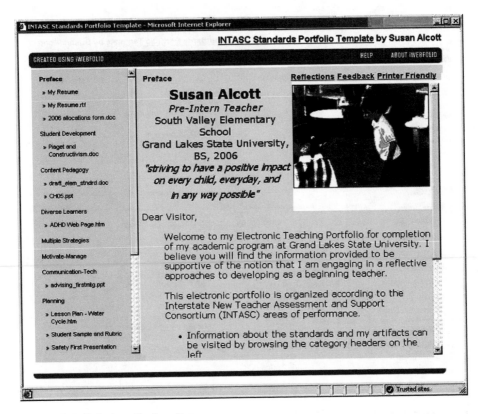

FIGURE 7.1 Introductory Page

individual expression and participation in all realms, it is not surprising that the idea of building portfolios is quickly taking root across the globe. In some European countries, there is discussion of a goal of every individual having his or her own portfolio.[3]

What does this mean in concrete terms for a teacher candidate learning to build a portfolio? In a nutshell, even though portfolio use is still being defined, and best practices are only just beginning to be established, as a participant in the portfolio process you will be an early adopter in what is becoming a universal tool across disciplines. Build your portfolio wisely and invest yourself in its bounty. As you can see, it is not a short-term goal but a lifelong practice. In the next section, we look at samples of artifacts from pre-service and professional electronic teacher portfolios.

ELECTRONIC PORTFOLIO ARTIFACTS

The first part of this section is a sneak peek into the pre-service portfolio of a hypothetical candidate, Susan Alcott. On the left you see a navigation pane showing links to various parts of the portfolio. The template used is one

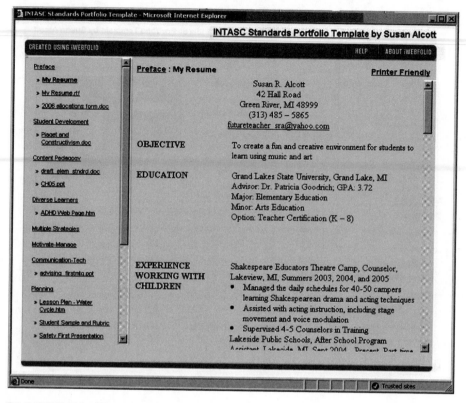

FIGURE 7.2 Résumé

based on INTASC standards, and these standards are headings on the navigation pane. Artifacts attached under different headings are visible as well. The portfolio reviewer is free to select the order in which he or she will examine Susan's artifacts.

The second part, serving as an in-service example, is a brief glimpse of the tenure and promotion portfolio of Royce Robertson (a.k.a. "portfolio guy" from Plymouth State University). He shares his mission statement and a service artifact. Again, the navigation pane on the left is a reviewer-friendly feature.

Pre-service Examples

Susan's message to her reviewers invites feedback from them, and shows how easy it would be to provide feedback by clicking on the link (Figure 7.1). She indicates that additional information on standards is also available. The picture on the top right provides the motif of an active classroom, supported by the other parts of her portfolio.

Susan's résumé has a clear objective that supports her role as a teacher and is tailored to share the experiences she believes are vital to her candidacy: her work with children using music and art (Figure 7.2). Her artifacts reveal her ability to

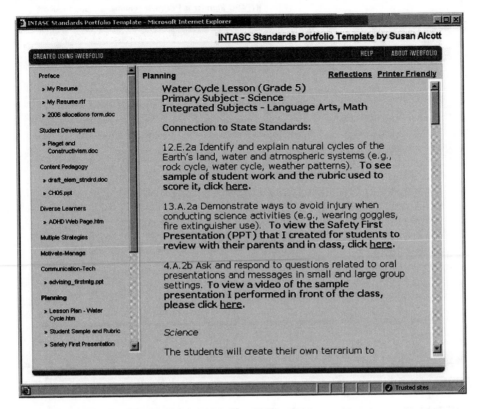

FIGURE 7.3 Lesson Plan

make difficult subjects fun by presenting them in ways children find interesting and enjoyable.

Here's a lesson plan that shows Susan's ability to adhere to state standards, as well as get parents involved. There is a Microsoft PowerPoint® presentation and a video of her presentation skills attached to the portfolio, which can be viewed by her reviewers then and there. This is followed by a narrative about the activities undertaken by her students (Figure 7.3).

The reflection shared by Susan is an honest representation of her true feelings about her own teaching experiences. It clearly reveals that she is learning from her experiences and thinking about them (Figure 7.4).

The Self Rate portion of the portfolio underscores the developmental nature of the teaching process. The rubric helps provide the candidate with guidelines for growth and improvement. This activity is a great way for candidates to measure their own skills and will provide good benchmarks further along in the program (Figure 7.5).

The reviewer's feedback is a particularly helpful feature of this electronic portfolio. Having the ability to capture feedback then and there, and save it for future reference, allows both portfolio owners and reviewers to maximize the value of the communication between them (Figure 7.6).

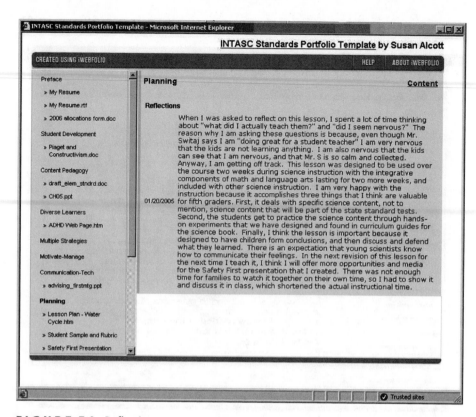

FIGURE 7.4 Reflection

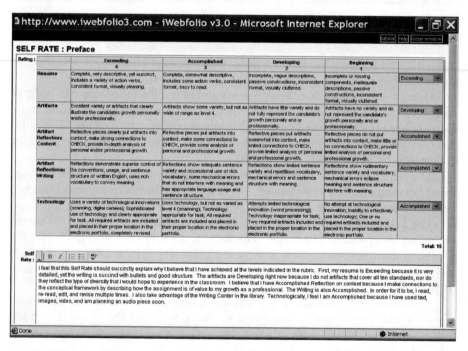

FIGURE 7.5 Self Rate

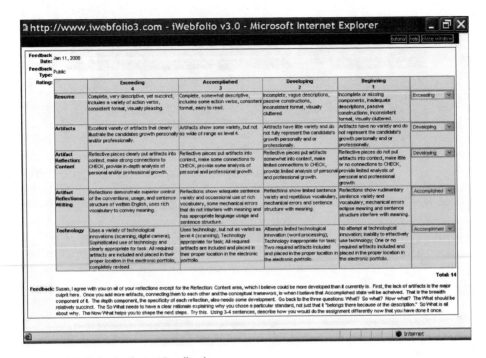

FIGURE 7.6   Reviewer Feedback

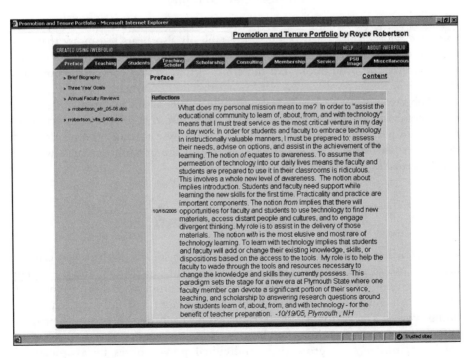

FIGURE 7.7   Mission Statement

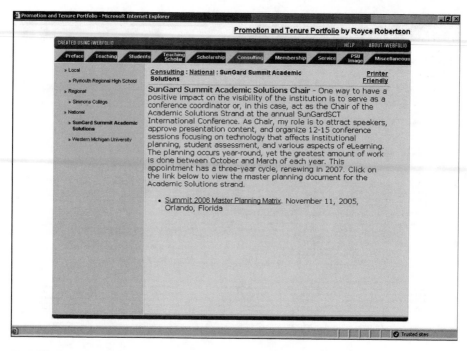

FIGURE 7.8 Service Artifact

Professional Examples

Robertson's reflection on his mission is indicative of the mature reflection process that in-service professionals bring to the table. It also bears testimony that as a teacher, one never stops reflecting. Royce's commitment and mission are crucial to his tenure and promotion, and therefore form a central part of the portfolio (Figure 7.7).

Robertson shares a service artifact from his career and is able to provide a link to further evidence of his efforts. Instead of being forced to go through documentation in a particular order, the reviewer can browse through the portfolio as desired. At the same time, concrete evidence of the portfolio owner's work is readily available (Figure 7.8).

LOOKING FORWARD

In Chapter 2, we mentioned the ideal of a learning society. Perhaps you can see how the use of the portfolio as a tool for assessing individual and collective growth can contribute to this ideal. To achieve a common goal, every member of the team must share the dream and commitment and fully participate in doing what it takes to make the goal a reality. Each person brings their own unique set of strengths, their own histories and perspectives. We need a way to celebrate, utilize, and grow these individual powerhouses by a process of communication and knowledge transfer that is mutually enriching and beneficial to everyone. The use of tools such as the portfolio (reaping the technological advantages of using its electronic format where available) holds the potential to turn these ideals into reality.

Now it is time to get back to the exciting task you have begun. Get ready to tell your story. The world is listening.

ENDNOTES

1. Xu, J. (2003, September–October). *Journal of Teacher Education.* Retrieved December 29, 2005, from http://infotrac.thomsonlearning.com.

2. Wolf, K. (1996, March). *Educational Leadership.* Retrieved December 29, 2005, from http://infotrac.thomsonlearning.com.

3. Retrieved December 10, 2005, from http://www.eife-l.org/eifel/about/.

Appendix

iWebfolio

OVERVIEW

How does an individual share the knowledge and understanding gained throughout life with teachers, peers, employers, friends, and family? What details are available to reveal the depth of educational and professional experience? How has a person been shaped by events in life and what evidence exists of accomplishments?

Individuals and institutions are demanding electronic portfolio management solutions to help archive, organize, reflect, and present information contained in documents, graphics, presentations, Web projects, audio and video, or any other digital media.

With iWebfolio, you can create an unlimited number of portfolio views and dynamically share them with anyone, including faculty, peers, admissions departments, colleagues, or potential employers. You can add reflections and share your insights about each piece of work. Faculty members and others given access to a portfolio can review, rate, and provide feedback about your work, creating a positive and collaborative learning experience.

iWebfolio also provides you with a way to demonstrate your personal and professional achievements. Portfolios can be used to document formal and continuing education, community service, as well as any other skills and accomplishments. Samples of work can demonstrate abilities and showcase special talent. Any number of portfolios can be created, and access to each can be provided to specific people for review. And *you* are in control of who views your content and for how long. A record of access enables you to know who has reviewed each portfolio by date.

CREATING YOUR iWEBFOLIO ACCOUNT

The iWebfolio access card included with this book can be used to create and set up an iWebfolio account. Once your account is activated, you can begin creating as many portfolios as you wish. Your account will have **50MB** of storage space for you to upload samples of your work.

During the sign-up process you will be asked for an "affiliation code." This code will affiliate your iWebfolio account to a particular institution. Once affiliated to the institution, you will be able to use templates created by that institution. For example, if you wish to use an INTASC standards template as mentioned in the body of this book, you must first affiliate to an institution that has created an INTASC standards template. Check with your instructor to find out if your institution has created templates and if an affiliation code exists. If you do not know the affiliation code at the time of sign-up, you may affiliate to your institution after your account has been created.

Note: For individual users not affiliated with an institution, please skip step 2.

1. Go to www.iwebfolio.com and click the **sign up now!** button to start the sign-up process.

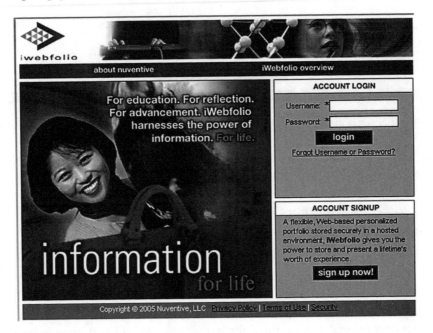

2. Enter your affiliation code if you have one.
3. Enter the information requested for your new account. You will be able to change your password once your account is created; however, you *will not* be able to change your username. In addition, make sure the email address you enter is valid. If you forget your password, the password will only be sent to the email address that is on file. Click **Next.** Select **iWebfolio Registration Card** from the drop-down menu. Enter the serial number and registration code that appear on your iWebfolio card. Click **Next.** Note: You

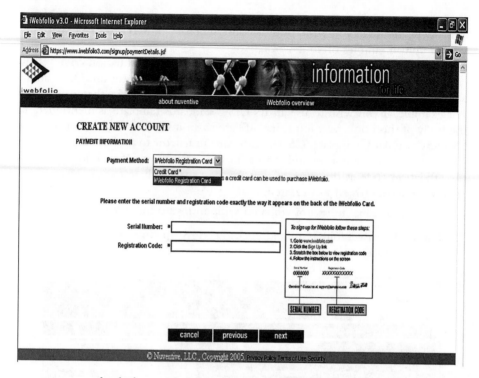

must enter both the serial number and registration code exactly as they appear on the card.

Note: For users not affiliated with an institution, you will be creating a portfolio from scratch. If you are using a template, the on-line tutorial for building a portfolio based upon a template will provide helpful information.

4. Click **Go to iWebfolio** and log in using the username and password you specified during sign-up.

GETTING STARTED

Once you log into iWebfolio, there are two tutorials that will help you get started: an overview tutorial and a tutorial for building portfolios based upon templates.

In addition to the tutorials, the on-line help addresses frequently asked questions about all the primary functions of iWebfolio. The tutorials and the on-line help are located in the upper-right corner of the iWebfolio screen.

STEP 1: CREATING A NEW PORTFOLIO

1. Click the **My Portfolios** link in the left navigation bar.
2. Click the **Create New Portfolio** link near the top center of the screen. You will be asked whether you would like to base the portfolio on a template.

3. Select the option **No** from the drop-down menu and click **Next** to continue.

4. At the prompts, provide your first and last name, the portfolio name, and the portfolio description. Your name will be filled in with the information from your profile. You must provide a portfolio name.

5. Click **Save**. You will be taken to the edit portfolio screen where you can begin adding artifacts.

STEP 2: ADDING CATEGORIES TO YOUR PORTFOLIO

Categories within a portfolio serve as a table of contents by grouping similar artifacts you have attached to the portfolio. Reviewers will see a list of these categories when they view your portfolio and can use the categories to help navigate within the portfolio. For example, you may create a category named "Skills" to which you would attach artifacts that demonstrate and/or explain your skills.

Portfolios must have at least one category. You may create as many categories within a portfolio as you like. When you create a new portfolio, a category named "Home" is included by default. You can rename this category as described under "Editing a Category" below. You can change the order of categories as described under "Reordering Categories."

If you created the portfolio from a template, some categories may be read-only, and their sequence cannot be changed. Categories you add are placed after the template categories and cannot be reordered.

Adding a New Category

1. Click the **My Portfolios** link in the left navigation bar.

2. Click the **Edit** link to the right of the portfolio you wish to change.

3. Click the **CONTENTS** tab in the upper part of the screen.

4. Click the **Add New Category** link above the list of categories at the left of the screen.

5. Provide the **Category Name** where prompted. The category name should be short and meaningful to help reviewers navigate your portfolio (e.g., Skills, Hobbies, Experience).

6. In the large text box below the category name, create the content you would like reviewers to see when they click on the category. You can use the category toolbar to format the category content.

For example, for a category named Skills you may want to provide a general description of your skills. Remember that you can then attach artifacts to this category that demonstrate and explain your skills further.

7. To save the category and continue working on the category content, click the **Save & Continue** button. When you are finished, click the **Save & Return** button to go back to the previous screen.

Editing a Category

1. Click the **My Portfolios** link in the left navigation bar.
2. Click the **Edit** link to the right of the portfolio you wish to change.
3. Click the **CONTENTS** tab in the upper part of the screen.
4. On the left side of the portfolio, click the name of the category you wish to edit. Any content associated with the category will be displayed.
5. Click the **Edit** link in the upper right of the screen. The **Edit** link will be disabled if the selected category was marked as read-only in the template used to create the portfolio.
6. Edit the name and content for the category as needed. You can use the category toolbar to format the category content.
7. To save your changes and continue editing the category, click the **Save & Continue** button. When you are finished editing, click the **Save & Return** button to go back to the previous screen.

Reordering Categories

1. Click the **My Portfolios** link in the left navigation bar.
2. Click the **Edit** link to the right of the portfolio you wish to change.
3. Click the **CONTENTS** tab in the upper part of the screen.
4. In the list of categories at the left of the screen, use the small arrows next to each category name to move that category up or down. The arrows will be disabled and reordering prohibited if the categories were marked as read-only in the template used to create the portfolio.

Deleting a Category

1. Click the **My Portfolios** link in the left navigation bar.
2. Click the **Edit** link to the right of the portfolio you wish to change.
3. Click the **CONTENTS** tab in the upper part of the screen.
4. On the left side of the portfolio, click the name of the category you wish to delete. Any content associated with the category will be displayed.
5. Click the **Remove** link in the upper right of the screen. The category will be deleted from the portfolio.

Note that deleting a category will not delete the artifacts you have attached to the category. They will remain in your **My Files**, **My Items**, or **My Websites**, and they may be attached to other categories and portfolios.

STEP 3: ATTACHING ARTIFACTS TO YOUR PORTFOLIO CATEGORIES

Artifacts may include Files, Items, or Websites. When you choose to add a new artifact to your iWebfolio account, you will select whether it is an existing digital File you will upload, an Item you will create within iWebfolio, or the home page address of a Website you have uploaded into iWebfolio. Artifacts you attach to your portfolios are stored within the appropriate section: **My Files**, **My Items**, or **My Websites**. This allows you to use the same artifact in multiple portfolios.

The arrangement of artifacts within your portfolio is determined by where you attach the artifact. For example, if you have a file that provides evidence or support for another file, you may attach the new file under the existing file in your portfolio. The new item will be indented under the existing file to show the connection.

Adding a File

1. Click the **My Portfolios** link in the left navigation bar.
2. Click the **Edit** link to the right of the portfolio you wish to change.
3. Click the **CONTENTS** tab in the upper part of the screen.
4. Click the category or item from the left to which you want to attach the file. The item you select will be presented with an **Attachments** tab along the bottom.
5. Select the **Attachments** tab and click the **Add Attachment** link at the right. A pop-up screen appears in which you select the artifact to attach.

Note that the link will be disabled if the template used to create the portfolio has restricted attachments to the category or item you selected. If the link is disabled, you may not attach files to that particular category or item.

6. Select the option **File** from the **Add** drop-down menu. The screen will display the contents of your **My Files** section.

    To attach a file previously uploaded to iWebfolio:

7. Click on the name of the folder containing the file you wish to add. The list of files within a folder is displayed to the right of the folder list.
8. To view a file before selecting it, click the **View** link to the right of that file. When you have found the file you want to use, click the **Attach** link.

    To attach a file not previously uploaded to iWebfolio:

7. Click the **Add New File** link.
8. Click the **Browse** button and navigate to the file on your computer that you wish to upload.

9. Click the **Save File(s)** button to upload the file.

10. Once the file has uploaded, click the **Attach** link to the right of the file.

Adding a Website

1. Click the **My Portfolios** link in the left navigation bar.

2. Click the **Edit** link to the right of the portfolio you wish to change.

3. Click the **CONTENTS** tab in the upper part of the screen.

4. Click the category or item from the left to which you want to attach the file. The item you select will be presented with an **Attachments** tab along the bottom.

5. Select the **Attachments** tab and click the **Add Attachment** link at the right. A pop-up screen appears in which you select the artifact to attach.

Note that the link will be disabled if the template used to create the portfolio has restricted attachments to the category or item you selected. If the link is disabled, you may not attach files to that particular category or item.

6. Select the option **Website** from the **Add** drop-down menu. The screen will display the contents of your **My Websites** section.

To attach a Website previously uploaded to iWebfolio:

7. To view a Website before selecting it, click the **View** link to the right of that Website. When you have found the Website you want to use, click the **Attach** link.

To attach a Website not previously uploaded to iWebfolio:

7. Click the **Upload New Website** link. A pop-up screen appears with prompts for information about the Website.

8. Enter a name for the Website. Click the **Browse** button and navigate to the .zip archive file on your computer that contains the Website you wish to upload.

9. Click the **Save** button to upload the Website.

10. Once the Website has uploaded, click the **Attach** link to the right of the file.

Adding an Item

1. Click the **My Portfolios** link in the left navigation bar.

2. Click the **Edit** link to the right of the portfolio you wish to change.

3. Click the **CONTENTS** tab in the upper part of the screen.

4. Click the category or item from the left to which you want to attach the file. The item you select will be presented with an **Attachments** tab along the bottom.

5. Select the **Attachments** tab and click the **Add Attachment** link at the right. A pop-up screen appears in which you select the artifact to attach.

Note that the link will be disabled if the template used to create the portfolio has restricted attachments to the category or item you selected. If the link is disabled, you may not attach files to that particular category or item.

6. Select the option **Item** from the **Add** drop-down menu. The screen will display the contents of your **My Items** section.

To attach an item previously created in iWebfolio:

7. Click on the name of the folder containing the item you wish to add. The list of items within a folder is displayed to the right of the folder list.

8. To view an item before selecting it, click the **View** link to the right of that item. When you have found the item you want to use, click the **Attach** link.

To attach an item not previously created in iWebfolio:

7. Click the **Add New Item** link. A screen appears with prompts for information about the item.

8. Provide the **Item Name** where prompted. The name should be short, meaningful, and describe what is in the item (e.g., Contact Information, Computer Skills, Vacation Pictures, etc.).

9. Provide any **Comments/Notes** you wish to make about the item where prompted. The comments will not be displayed in your portfolio but will be viewable by you in the future.

10. In the large text box, create the content you would like reviewers to see when they click on the item. You can use the item toolbar to format the item content.

For example, if your item name was Skills, you may want to insert a table and describe each of your skills. In addition to typing text, you can use the toolbar to format the text, add color, provide links to files you have already uploaded into iWebfolio, or insert thumbnail images.

11. To save the item and continue working on the item content, click the **Save & Continue** button. When you are finished, click the **Save & Return** button to go back to the previous screen.

12. Once the item has created, click the **Attach** link to the right of the item.

STEP 4: SELECTING A PRESENTATION STYLE

1. Click the **My Portfolios** link in the left navigation bar.

2. Click the **Edit** link to the right of the portfolio you wish to change.

3. Click the **PRESENTATION** tab in the upper part of the screen.

4. You may click on any of the images to see a sample of what the presentation style will look like. Select the style you like by clicking in the circle below the

desired style. Note: After you select a style, you can see what your portfolio looks like with that style by clicking on **View Portfolio** in the upper-right corner of the screen.

STEP 5: GIVING ACCESS TO OTHERS TO VIEW YOUR PORTFOLIO

Each portfolio can be shared with a different set of reviewers. There are two types of reviewers: Affiliated Reviewers and Custom Reviewers. **Affiliated Reviewers** are reviewers associated with your institution (e.g., faculty members). Affiliated Reviewers will be listed for you in the permission tree. **Custom Reviewers** are reviewers outside of your institution (e.g., potential employers). To add a custom reviewer, see the **How do I add a Custom Reviewer?** on-line help topic. If your portfolio was built from a template, default permissions may have been established. As the portfolio owner, you always have the option of removing permissions for any portfolio.

Granting Permission to an Affiliated Reviewer

1. Click the **My Portfolios** link in the left navigation bar.
2. Click the **Edit** link to the right of the portfolio you wish to change.
3. Click the **PERMISSIONS** tab in the upper part of the screen.
4. In the **Permissions** section of the screen, select your institution from the drop-down menu.
5. Navigate through the list of nodes on the left to locate the node containing the reviewer to whom you wish to grant permissions. Click on the node name to display the list of reviewers within that node on the right.

Note that a node can be expanded to display subnodes by clicking on the arrow to the left of the node name. The Expand All link can also be used to display all nodes and subnodes under the institution.

6. Mark the checkbox next to the name of each reviewer to whom you wish to grant permissions.
7. Click the **Save** button. A pop-up screen appears to confirm your selection.
8. Click the **OK** button to confirm the selection. The screen will display the reviewers in the **Current Permissions** section as having access to your portfolio.

Granting Permission to a Custom Reviewer

1. Click the **My Portfolios** link in the left navigation bar.
2. Click the **Edit** link to the right of the portfolio you wish to change.

3. Click the **PERMISSIONS** tab in the upper part of the screen.

4. In the **Permissions** section of the screen, select **Custom Reviewers** from the drop-down menu.

5. Click the **Give Permission** link to the right of the reviewer to whom you wish to grant permissions. A pop-up screen appears to confirm your selection.

6. Click the **OK** button to confirm the selection. A pop-up screen appears with prompts for information about the reviewer access.

7. You may set the reviewer's access to expire on a specific date, limit the reviewer to a specific number of accesses, or both by providing values at the specified prompts. You may also change the default subject and message that is sent to inform the reviewer that permission has been granted to your portfolio. Click the **Preview Email** button to view the message.

Note that the email will contain a link to your portfolio. If you remove permission for the Custom Reviewer, the link in the email will become invalid and the custom reviewer will no longer be able to view the portfolio. In order to grant the reviewer access again, you must send another email to them by clicking the **Give Permission** link.

8. Click the **Send Email** button to send the message to the reviewer, or click the **Cancel** button if you do not wish to send the message at this time. The pop-up screen will close automatically.

Removing Permission from a Reviewer

1. Click the **My Portfolios** link in the left navigation bar.

2. Click the **Edit** link to the right of the portfolio you wish to change.

3. Click the **PERMISSIONS** tab in the upper part of the screen.

4. The **Current Permissions** section of the screen displays the list of all reviewers who have been granted permission to the portfolio. Click the **Remove** link to the right of the reviewer name to remove permissions for that reviewer.